DEATH VISITS A BAWDY HOUSE

A CHARLOTTE EDGERTON MYSTERY

Adele Fasick

MonganBooks

SAN FRANCISCO, CALIFORNIA

Book Layout ©2013 BookDesignTemplates.com

Cover design by Kit Foster Design.

Death Visits a Bawdy House/ Adele Fasick. -- 1st ed.
ISBN 978-0-9853152-3-8

In memory of my mother and father and all the other immigrants who braved the rigors of New York City

CHAPTER ONE

Charlotte Arrives in Manhattan

A million people—manners free and superb—open voices—hospitality—
the most courageous and friendly young men;
City of hurried and sparkling waters! City of spires and masts!
City nested in bays! My city!

Saturday, November 11, 1843

As the ship moved closer toward shore passengers crowded around the rail. The buildings of New York started to appear in the dim early morning light. Black smoke from a tall chimney on shore streamed across the gray sky. Charlotte pushed forward to watch sailing ships flitting down the East River straining to stay out of the way of the heavy wake left by their steamship as it headed doggedly upriver.

"No need to shove, young lady," rasped a voice at her elbow. She turned to see a short, stocky man wearing a green corduroy jacket. He smiled at her and winked his eye. "Looking for your sweetheart, are you? A pretty girl like you shouldn't have to wait for anyone."

1

Charlotte turned away, pretending not to hear. But the surging crowd pinned her between the railing and the over-familiar man. He touched her arm as if to lead her to a less crowded spot and continued talking.

"I've noticed you ever since we left Boston. Might you be looking for a room in New York? My sister keeps a very reputable boarding house. I'll be glad to introduce you to her. Nothing but young ladies in her house, all very respectable and cozy."

"No, thank you," answered Charlotte. "My cousin will be meeting me. I have no need of introductions." She felt her cheeks grow hot as she turned away. Daniel wasn't really her cousin, but she had to make this man understand that she was a respectable young lady and his advances were unwelcome.

As the man tipped his battered hat to her and pushed ahead toward the gangplank, Charlotte slipped her hand in her pocket and felt the creased paper of Daniel's latest letter. "The days go slowly while I wait for you to arrive," he had written. The days had moved slowly for her too. It was six long months since she had seen him. Would he look different? Had life in the big city changed him at all?

The trip from Boston had lasted only a day and a half, very different from the eight-week voyage across the Atlantic when Charlotte sailed into Boston five years ago. She had been young and frightened then, but she had not regretted leaving England and the poverty her family suffered there. She had found friends in Boston and lost some of them too. Best of all she had found Daniel, another young immigrant, who had left Ireland to find a new life. Daniel was ambitious and so was she. Now, at 25, they were both ready for a larger city and a new life.

New York looked and sounded more alive than Boston. The sky was overhung with smoke, the engines of the steamships churned noisily, and the shouts of peddlers and hawkers on shore sounded clearly across the water. The cart horses stamped their feet as fearless rats scurried underfoot snatching scraps of food. As the ship nosed toward a dock, Charlotte searched the waiting crowd to find Daniel. There he was! His dark hair was whipped by the wind as he waved his cap. A jolt of joy made her heart beat faster. And then she realized he was not alone. A young woman wearing a black dress and a bonnet trimmed with yellow flowers was beside him peering up toward the passengers on deck.

Charlotte tapped her foot impatiently as the ship was tied up to the dock and the gangplank went down. Then it was push and shove with the rest of the passengers toward the dock, her worn satchel clutched in her hand. Men in top hats and women in fancy bonnets jostled for position just as hard as the workmen and women; everyone was eager to leave the cramped ship. Finally Charlotte was on the gangplank and two minutes later headed straight toward Daniel. He reached out to grasp her hand, took her satchel, and turned toward the girl at his side.

"Eileen, this is Charlotte Edgerton. You've heard me speak of her. My sister, Eileen Gallagher."

Daniel's sister had a thin, pale face and dark blue eyes, her smile was cheerful as she said, "Good day to you, Miss Edgerton. Daniel has told me a lot about you and I'm glad to meet you for myself."

"And I am happy to meet you, Miss Gallagher. I did not know that you were in New York already."

"I landed two weeks ago, so I am almost an old-timer in the city now. Daniel has been showing me all the sights."

Daniel went off to collect Charlotte's small trunk while the women waited on the cobblestone street beside the dock. The wind was fresh and the smell of fish hung in the salt air. Charlotte could hear the slapping of water against the dock and the sound of many languages— German and French, and some lilting language she couldn't identify.

"Are you looking for employment in the city, Miss Gallagher?" Charlotte asked.

Eileen beamed with pleasure. "I have already found a position with a grand family up on Washington Square. A young man who works with Daniel has an aunt who heard that the Van Pelts were losing one of their maids and were looking for someone to fill the place. I was fortunate that Daniel's friend persuaded her to recommend me to Mrs. Van Pelt. Daniel's employer, Mr. Greeley, gave me a letter of reference too. I am only an under-maid, but I am willing to learn and I hope to rise fast. Daniel says that is possible here in America."

Daniel soon appeared carrying Charlotte's small trunk. "Now I will show you the boarding house where you can live for a while until you know the city better. Eileen stayed there for a few days before she found employment. The house is just up the street from where I board and has a reputation as a safe place that takes only women as boarders. Your new employers at the African school will approve and I think you will like living there while you settle into your teaching position."

The three of them walked to the boarding house on Thomas Street, and then Daniel left to return to his work at the newspaper office. Charlotte and Eileen sat down in the quiet parlor for a chat after he had gone. A gloomy enough room it was, with murky green walls and dark mahogany furniture. The windows were hung with heavy velvet drapes and ecru curtains that kept out most of the light from the street. But a dark room couldn't dim Charlotte's spirits; she was excited about being in New York, close to Daniel and with a job promised to her.

Eileen sounded cheerful too as she told Charlotte about her experiences since coming to New York. "For years I've been trying to save money so I could follow Daniel to America, but it was slow going, a penny at a time, until Daniel sent me money to add to what I had saved. I thought our mother should be the first one to come over, but both she and Daniel insisted that I take the money. My mother says that when she has two children working in America then she will feel perfectly safe in coming over.

"I'm so proud of Daniel. That nice Mr. Greeley thinks he is a fine reporter and encourages him to write all about the politics in this city. And believe me there's a lot to write. This city is amazing. It's filled with wicked people the likes of which I've never seen in Galway. I've passed by painted women going up and down Broadway in broad daylight. And do you know, the policemen just smile and tip their hats to them? Such scandalous behavior and right on the main street. But no one even seems to notice." Charlotte told Eileen about the man on the ship who had accosted her. They agreed that rather than hiding its shady side, New York seemed to flaunt its reputation as Sin City.

When Eileen left to go back to her work, Charlotte decided to make her escape from the quiet house and take a walk to explore the city. The first thing she noticed was that New York streets were dirtier than the ones in Boston. Scraps of paper blew down the wide stretch of Broadway, trampled by the dozens of people walking. Both men and women pushed their way through the crowds, scrambling to avoid the hackney cabs and coaches that took up the center of the street. Most remarkable of all were the pigs, strolling along underfoot, snuffling for scraps of garbage and paying no attention to people. Charlotte saw women in dresses of every color—bright blue, green, and gleaming maroon. Some of the men were colorful too, with their blue coats studded with bright brass buttons. Negro coachmen wore fancy straw hats or black caps and red jackets.

She didn't mean to stay out long, but wandered down Broadway as far as she could absorbing the lively sights and sounds. The sky was growing darker with storm clouds rolling in, but she was busy looking at the swarm of people on the streets. The further she went the more the crowds thickened. She was swept along in the direction everyone was going until she came upon a remarkable building. Banners fluttered in the breeze over the wide doorway and a huge sign proclaimed "American Museum".

Charlotte stared at the signs outside the building: "See the famous Figi mermaid"; "genuine flea circus"; "wild animals"; "only 25 cents!" Outside the entrance, a line of people slowly progressed to the ticket seller at the door and then disappeared inside. Spending money on a peep show wasn't something Charlotte could do right now, but New York certainly was full of people who had money and time.

A loud clap of thunder made Charlotte jump. Rain came pelting down, slowly at first, but gradually getting heavier. Two brilliantly dressed young women, whose cheeks were rosy with paint, had come out of the museum and were strolling up Broadway. As the rain started they began to run and Charlotte followed close behind them. To her surprise they made their way to Thomas Street, to the very block where her boarding house stood. They disappeared into a large house directly across the street from where she was staying. Charlotte couldn't help wondering what it would be like to live so close to where these women lived. They certainly did not look like respectable young women who led quiet lives.

Daniel was waiting for her when she arrived and was eager to tell her about his plans and all the places he wanted to take her.

"I want to see all the sights in New York. I've heard so much about what an exciting city this is with theaters and art galleries. This afternoon I caught a glimpse of P. T. Barnum's American Museum. But first of all I want to meet the teachers and the children I will be teaching. I've never met many free blacks."

"Your new school will be very different from the school at Brook Farm," Daniel agreed. "Everything is different in New York. Oh, we are going to have a wonderful time in this city. I'm sure of it. We will both have new lives."

Despite her excitement, Charlotte soon found she was so tired she could barely keep her eyes open. When she finally got to her small room on the top floor, she was asleep before she knew it.

****

A sudden bang jolted Charlotte awake and she stared around the room for a minute. Then she heard the sound of breaking glass. She pushed aside her quilt and ran to the window. Below in the street she saw several men pushing their way into a house across the street—the same house the two women had entered earlier that day. Through the open door she could see a fire blazing in the fireplace and people's faces reflected in the mirror above it. Those people certainly kept late hours.

What in heaven's name could be going on? There seemed to be a fight of some sort. She gasped as one man lifted a heavy cudgel and smashed the mirror. The glittering shards of glass flew off the wall above the fireplace.

Passers-by were gathering on the street outside. Why were so many people out on the street in the middle of the night? Men shoved and laughed as they looked through the open door at the scene beyond. Then a few men started retreating out of the door and back onto the street. In the doorway Charlotte saw a heavyset woman brandishing an iron skillet. She struck one of the men a blow on the head and he reeled down the steps and into the arms of one of his friends behind him. The door was slammed shut, leaving the men outside muttering and shuffling. Gradually the noise subsided and the crowd dispersed. One man lifted his arm and shook his fist at the house that had shut them out. He looked as though he was planning to return and attack again.

Charlotte realized how tired she was and retreated to bed, but she had trouble falling asleep. Every sound made her jump; the quiet whisk of a mouse scuttling behind the wardrobe seemed ominous. Even after the street outside grew quiet again, it was noisier than her old home in Massachusetts. At Brook Farm only the occasional bark of a dog in the distance had ever broken the stillness. What kind of place was she in now where people shouted in the night? This new world was fast moving and dangerous. Was she ready to take it on?

CHAPTER TWO

Sporting House Life

Lady of beauty, frail yet fair,
Devoted to the shrine of folly,
Though decked in jewels rich and rare,
Thy life will close in melancholy.

Sunday, November 12, 1843

Charlotte woke early on Sunday morning eager to explore her new city. Daniel had promised he would come to see her as early as a man could decently call on a young woman. Eileen too would visit when she had finished her chores at the Van Pelts.

When she went downstairs for breakfast, Charlotte was disappointed to find a note from Daniel saying he would be late. Eileen however arrived as soon as the first mass was over and the two set out on a walk in the crisp November air. As they sauntered down Broadway, watching hansom cabs carrying prosperous families to church, Charlotte told Eileen about the late night disturbance at the house across the street. Eileen nodded her head and whispered that she was sure the house was a brothel.

"You have no idea how many of those there are in a city like New York. They call them sporting houses. Ladies aren't supposed to know anything about them, but the truth is I have met one of the women who lives in that very house." Eileen lowered her voice as she continued.

"A few days after I had started working, when I went to the kitchen to have my meal with the staff after the family had finished theirs, I found a visitor there. She was Susan, a former maid in the house. She was dressed in a lovely blue gown and I thought she must have married a successful man. Daniel is always telling me that's what maidservants can do in America.

"That evening was especially cheerful. Susan sang us a song and a lovely one it was. Something about 'endearing young charms'. I thought she was a lucky woman to be wearing a gorgeous dress and learning such beautiful songs. But I soon changed my mind."

"What happened? It certainly sounds as though she was doing well for herself." Charlotte was all ears.

"I noticed that when she got up from the table and stepped into the pantry, the footman put his arm around her in a very familiar way. I was near the door and I heard the footman tell her he would walk her back to her house that night if he could slip away from the master. And when we heard footsteps coming down the stairs from the dining room, Susan turned and ran out the kitchen door and disappeared so fast I was astonished. It was only Mrs. Van Pelt come to compliment Cook on the meal, but I wondered why Susan would be so afraid of her."

"Did you find out why she was scared?"

"Later that night when Molly, the other maid who shares my room, and I went upstairs, she told me Susan had been a maid for the Van Pelts but she had gotten herself into trouble. For a long time she didn't tell anyone, but Molly started to have her suspicions when Susan began to get fat and look sick in the morning. Molly's not a babe in the woods and she knew it wouldn't be long before Mrs. Van Pelt found out. Oh there was a fuss when she did! Susan was sent packing and Molly was sure she would never see her again."

"Was she thrown out on the street?" Charlotte could imagine how dreadful that would be in a crowded, dirty city. "Where would she go?"

Eileen leaned closer to Charlotte. "Everyone thought she'd have no place to go. Cook and Molly told her to come back to the kitchen door if she needed food. They were worried. But Susan was cool as a cucumber and said she'd go back to her family up in Schenectady. She said she was sure her mother would take her in. Molly never heard anything for more than a year.

"Then one day when Molly was walking up Broadway on her half day off who did she see but Susan, strolling along looking pleased with herself? She was wearing a pink dress and carrying a white parasol just like a lady.

But it's not a lady she had become, oh no! Far from it. She was living in a sporting house, she said, entertaining men and enjoying herself. And the baby? She had left him up in Schenectady with her sister who just dotes on him. She and her husband always wanted a boy, so the whole family is pleased by this arrangement."

Eileen looked bewildered by all the information Molly had given her. Charlotte felt confused too. She had always been told that girls who got into trouble led miserable lives. Didn't their babies suffer and wither away and often die young? New York seemed to turn the whole world upside-down. Had those two fashionable women Charlotte had seen the day before been girls like Susan? She decided she would keep a close eye on the house across the street. Not that she wanted to be a busybody, but it seemed sensible to try to understand what her neighbors were up to.

By the time Eileen and Charlotte returned to the boarding house, they were chatting like old friends. Eileen was able to stay at the boarding house for the noon meal, and soon after that Daniel arrived. He was full of news about the attack at the sporting house the night before.

"They call it a spree," he said, "when a bunch of men like that get together and decide to teach the women a lesson. Usually they've been drinking more than is good for them and they go from house to house causing damage in all the brothels."

"Do they want the women to reform?" asked Charlotte.

"Oh, I wouldn't say that," Daniel scoffed. "Sometimes it seems they just want revenge for having been tossed out of one of the houses for being disorderly. Or they are angry because they have so little money and the brothel keepers and the other women have beautiful furniture and far more dresses and jewelry than they need."

"Everything seems mixed up in New York," Charlotte pondered the strangeness of the news. "It's not the way the poet said, is it? *'When lovely woman stoops to folly'* she has to suffer and die. Here they get beautiful dresses and live in grand houses."

"Surely it can't be as simple as that," added Eileen. "Do you think Susan will always enjoy her life and be happy?"

"Perhaps I'll be able to find out," Daniel promised. "I am going to visit the house this afternoon and see how happy the place seems. I've already checked the newspaper files and found out that the house is owned by a Mrs. Alice Brown. Maybe she can tell me something about the men who broke in last night. It's too bad you can't come with me, but I'll tell the two of you what I find out."

A few minutes later Daniel walked across the street and knocked sharply on the door of Mrs. Brown's house. The door was opened by a short, middle-aged man wearing a bright green corduroy jacket.

"And what's your business, young man?" he asked in a raspy voice.

"I'm a reporter come to ask Mrs. Brown about the attack on her house last night. It's important to keep the public informed about unruly gangs that terrorize the people of our city."

"Ah, yes. I am Bert Brown and unfortunately I was away from home last night. My wife will speak with you soon, but at the moment we are having an entertainment in the parlor. Would you join us?"

Daniel was surprised to find that Alice Brown had a husband living in the house and he was curious about what kind of entertainment would be offered. A man's deep voice sounding rather theatrical was loud in the hallway. Daniel quickly accepted the invitation and walked into the parlor with Bert Brown.

It was a much more elegant room than the one in Charlotte's boarding house. A patterned carpet in deep wine color with a design of green leaves and pinecones covered the floor, several easy chairs with maroon upholstery were scattered around the room and over the large marble fireplace was a gold-framed mirror—or the remains of one. The mirror had only a few jagged shards of glass clinging to the backing, but the heavy gold frame must have made it an impressive piece before the glass was shattered.

Standing in front of the fireplace was a tall, thin man wearing a dark suit and holding a book in his hand. He looked up as Daniel and Mr. Brown entered, but paused only a moment in his reading. Three or four women and several men were spread around the room, sitting in the easy chairs or lounging on the rug. One pretty young girl with blonde curls was sitting in the lap of a portly man who caressed her curls with one hand while they both listened.

The sun had sunk, and the summer skies
Were dotted with specks of light,
That melted soon, in the deep moon-rise,
That flowed over Croton Height.
For the Evening, in her robe of white,
Smiled o'er sea and land, with pensive eyes,
Saddening the heart, like the first fair night
After a loved one dies.

An older woman, who seemed to be the hostess, noticed Daniel as he came in and spoke as soon as the poem had ended. "That's a sad poem for such a sunny day, but we thank you for sharing your poetry with us, Mr. Abington. Now I see we have another visitor."

Daniel cleared his throat as he looked around the room. He had planned on a quiet interview with Mrs. Brown and now everyone was looking at him as if they expected him to provide entertainment.

"I am a newspaper reporter, Mrs. Brown, and I was hoping to learn more about the unfortunate events of last night. People in this city are eager to stop the vandalism that has been occurring."

An eager chorus of voices broke in. One black-haired young lady in a brilliant blue dress started talking immediately. "Those men were drunk and disorderly. They pushed poor Mrs. Brown and almost knocked her down. But I showed them we are not weak women. I scratched one bully's face so hard I broke my fingernail and I warrant I left quite a mark on his cheek."

"And I recognized one of the men," said Mrs. Brown in an angry tone. "It was Francis O'Connor—or at least that's what he calls himself. And a rogue of an Irishman he is. He came to the door earlier, but he used such language as I've never heard before and I wouldn't let him in. I'm sure he came back out of spite to punish me." She turned and pointed at the mirror dramatically, "Just see what he has done to my lovely French mirror! I'll take him to court for damages. I promise you that."

"Did you call the watchman?" Daniel asked.

"I didn't have to call him. The man heard the noise and he came with two of the other watchmen from the neighborhood. They soon scattered the rascals whoever they were. There's lots of Irish troublemakers come off the boats every day. They're taking over the city. None of the troublemakers were caught so there's no charges been laid. I'll have to go down to the watch station and lay them myself."

Daniel wanted to strike back at that remark about the Irish being troublemakers, but he had to keep his job, so he held his tongue. Instead he turned to Mr. Abingdon. What was he doing in the house this afternoon? "Were you here last night, sir? Did you hear any of this?"

"No, I had been here earlier to pay a visit to Susan," Abington answered, turning with a smile to the young woman in the blue dress. "But I had left before any of the trouble started. I am a poet and often work through the night on my writing."

"Oh, and how could you leave poor Susan early?" teased a dark-haired woman in a red dress. "Everyone knows you're sweet on her."

The young blonde girl, safe in her gentleman's lap, giggled and stared pointedly at the woman in the blue dress. Daniel surmised that was Susan who said nothing but smiled serenely at the young poet.

A loud knocking on the door brought another caller, a tall, stout man in an expensive looking gray overcoat with a carefully curled mane of silver hair. He was accompanied by two young men with small mustaches and sleek walking sticks. When she saw the men enter, Mrs. Brown jumped to her feet to welcome them. She glanced quickly around as though looking for her husband, but he had disappeared.

"Welcome, Mayor Simpson, I am happy to see you in our salon. Mr. Abingdon was just reading some of his poetry to us. Would you care to hear more of it?"

Daniel moved back to a corner of the room the better to watch this scene. He had never met the mayor, although he had seen him walking from his City Hall offices occasionally. Once, when he tried to interview him about the new Croton Dam project, it had been impossible to get an appointment. "Mayor Simpson does not like to talk to reporters about city affairs," his young secretary said dismissively, stroking his silky mustache.

Doesn't like to talk to reporters indeed, Daniel thought to himself. He's afraid reporters will tell the city about some of Mayor Simpson's dealings with his friends in Tammany Hall. There were rumors that city licenses to construct new piers or to pave some of the new streets being laid out uptown were practically for sale by the mayor's cronies. Daniel had been living in New York for less than a year, but already he had heard far more scandal about the local politicians than he had during all the years he lived in Boston. Now he had a rare opportunity to observe the mayor in person.

Out of the corner of his eye Daniel saw the young blonde girl and her portly gentleman friend disappear up the stairs. Mrs. Brown showed the mayor to the chair in which they had been sitting.

"I understand that you were troubled by a rough gang of young men last night," the mayor said sympathetically. "The night watchmen's report says they caused quite a bit of damage before they were tossed out."

"Oh yes, indeed," Mrs. Brown's auburn curls were shaking with indignation. "They destroyed my lovely mirror and caused no end of trouble. Those ruffians ought to be in jail, but they were not even charged. They disappeared fast enough when the watchmen came, but I recognized a few of them and believe me, I intend to press charges."

"You should indeed press charges, madam," intoned the mayor. "We must maintain order in our city. I regret to say that some of my political opponents are determined to destroy many respectable business establishments. They are doing this in the name of morality, but where is the morality in destroying property and terrorizing women?"

He paused for effect, while Mrs. Brown and the other women nodded their heads in agreement.

"I must leave now. I trust you will not be bothered again by hooligans. Tell your fathers and brothers to vote for Mayor Simpson if they want to keep peace and order in our great city." With that, the mayor beckoned his two clerks and walked ponderously out of the room.

Daniel wondered whether it was really true that the spree last night had been a political trick played by the mayor's opponents. He had heard rumors about a movement to bring a new candidate to oppose the long-time mayor in the next election, but who would be brave enough to take on that challenge? It was time to delve a little deeper into New York politics and discover who the most powerful figures were. Mr. Greeley would surely want to uncover whatever corruption he could discover.

CHAPTER THREE

Charlotte Goes to School

Children are illuminated textbooks, breviaries of doctrine, living bodies of divinity, open always and inviting their elders to peruse the characters inscribed on the lovely leaves.

Monday, November 13, 1843

Charlotte left the boarding house early on Monday morning to meet John Fox, the director of the Pearl Street School for Africans, where she was to teach for the coming year. In his letter Mr. Fox had described how the school had been founded to provide education and religious training for children of the freed slaves in New York. "Far too many of the former slaves are illiterate", he wrote, and this is "a lingering symbol of their enslavement".

As she turned the corner into Pearl Street, Charlotte saw the two-story brick building. Large windows faced the street, and a triangular peak made the school resemble a church. When she got closer, she could hear the sound of young voices reciting familiar verses from the common reader. "A apple pie; B bit it; C cut it..."

Charlotte found John Fox in his bare office at the end of the central hallway. He was a small, brisk man wearing a sober dark suit. His spectacles glittered and he smiled as he rose from his chair.

"Ah, Miss Edgerton, I am glad to see you. I trust your journey from Boston was safe and comfortable. Let me show you around our school."

In the first classroom Charlotte saw a group of about twenty young girls, each clutching a piece of chalk and a wood-framed slate on which they were writing the letters of the alphabet. A tall, stately African woman was walking from chair to chair checking the accuracy of their writing. Across the hall was the boys' classroom presided over by a very young white man, hardly more than a boy, who was struggling to keep order. His young charges sat on long benches sharing their readers and poking one another whenever the teacher looked away. In one corner a sullen boy sat on a high stool wearing a sign reading "I must control my tongue".

After brief introductions, John Fox led the way back to his office. "I would like you to tell me what you know about the educational principles of Bronson Alcott," he said to Charlotte. "You are familiar with his work I understand, Miss Edgerton."

"I admire Mr. Alcott's work," she told him, "although I cannot say that I understand it completely. At Brook

Farm we believed that children, especially the youngest ones, learn best by being active in their learning rather than just sitting quietly and listening to their teachers. I always encouraged the children by singing songs with them and asking questions about their thoughts. That, I believe, has always been Bronson Alcott's method of education. For example…"

A thunderous rapping on the outside door interrupted Charlotte. She turned with surprise as she heard loud voices in the hallway. Then came a brisk knock on John Fox's office door, which was quickly opened to reveal two men who looked accustomed to giving orders. Both of them wore well-brushed and well-cut jackets and silky black cravats and both carried canes. One was a tall, broad-shouldered man with glossy chestnut hair, the other an African somewhat shorter and thinner than his companion. Both bowed slightly to acknowledge Charlotte's presence and then turned to John Fox.

"We are here to speak to you, sir, about a report made on the students at the last meeting of the Board's Education Committee," the black man spoke first. "But we will be glad to wait while you conclude your business with this young woman."

"Allow me to introduce Miss Charlotte Edgerton," responded John Fox. "She is a new teacher and will no doubt be interested in the report to which you refer."

"Miss Edgerton, this is Mr. Charles Bennett Ray, one of our board members," he said turning to the black man, "and Mr. Rex Hamilton, also a board member. Both are supporters of our school and have given invaluable help and advice. Now, gentlemen, perhaps you can tell both Miss Edgerton and myself about the report."

Mr. Ray addressed his audience in a quiet voice. "It has come to our attention that some of the trustees of the school have decided that Negro parents need to be educated about how to raise their children. It was suggested that the teachers—white teachers that is— should hold classes for parents to teach them 'morality and cleanliness'. His voice rose like that of a preacher addressing his congregation as he continued, "Cleanliness, sir! I beg to ask you whether the children who attend this school require help in meeting standards of cleanliness. Are they not suitably bathed and dressed? Pray tell me whether the parents who sacrifice themselves to enroll their children in school are not sufficiently aware of the standards of civilization to teach their own children about these matters."

Mr. Ray paused to allow an answer from John Fox, but Mr. Hamilton gave no time for an answer. In a thunderous voice he started. "We are losing support among the very people we have sworn to serve by publicly announcing these sentiments. I demand that some changes be made."

As he spoke, Rex Hamilton strode back and forth across the small office, holding his cane in one hand and swinging it rather recklessly around to emphasize his points. "As you may know," he continued, "I am running for the office of mayor of this city. Under my guidance, the city will provide a good education for all of our citizens. It is an important part of the reform agenda that I will propose."

"If you will allow me, sir" said John Fox meekly. "I am sure the remarks you have quoted do not reflect the thinking of most of our trustees. If you allow me, I will bring in one of our experienced teachers who may have something to add to the discussion."

He darted out of the room and soon returned with the tall African woman Charlotte had seen earlier in the classroom. "Gentlemen, I believe you know Mrs. Mercy Jackson who has been teaching in this school since its beginning."

Mrs. Jackson listened calmly to Charles Ray and Rex Hamilton as they repeated some of the words that had offended them. Then she spoke. "I assure you that this school respects its students and their parents. We are devoted to strengthening the education of all Negroes so they can take their places as free people in the great country of America."

John Fox took up the argument. "We are preparing our students for the day when the curse of slavery is lifted. Even though it no longer exists in New York State, it casts a dark shadow across all of us as long as it can be found anywhere in America. I am very glad to hear that it is an important part of your reform agenda, Mr. Hamilton."

Mercy Jackson nodded quietly in agreement as he spoke. Charles Ray, too, looked satisfied with Mr. Fox's declaration. Rex Hamilton still scowled as though he wanted to scold someone and when he spoke his voice was harsh.

"We must be sure to give every child in the city a good moral education. The boys need to be instructed in a trade so they will be able to provide food for themselves and their families. And the girls must learn their proper roles as wives and mothers. Our streets are disgraced by too many unmannerly and immoral people. Even very young women openly parade their sinful lives. My reform platform will ensure that our city becomes a decent place for respectable people to live." He bowed briefly to each of them and turned to leave. Mr. Ray smiled, nodded at the group, and followed him.

Charlotte was thoughtful as she finished her talk with Mr. Fox. She spent the rest of that first day in the girls' classroom. She watched while Mercy Jackson wrote familiar maxims on her large slate for the children to copy.

Don't count your chickens before they are hatched.

He laughs best who laughs last.

A penny saved is a penny earned.

Most of the girls wore faded dresses, many of which had patches on the skirt and bodice. The two youngest, perhaps five or six years old, clutched their slates tightly and frowned as they carefully traced the shape of each letter with their finger before committing it to chalk.

The oldest girls, who were probably fourteen or fifteen, also leaned over their slates, but they kept peering at Charlotte as she walked around the room. Were they wondering whether she would be their new teacher?

Charlotte had never been so close to a group of black people before. As they leaned over their slates, she studied their hair, twisted into tiny tight braids. She looked at the kinky black strands that escaped from the braids and wondered how the girls could ever brush their hair. No time to worry about hair now. Charlotte focused her attention on Mercy Jackson who was standing in front of the class.

Mrs. Jackson was an impressive figure, taller than Charlotte and with broad shoulders. She held a Bible in her strong, sinewy hands that looked more like a workingman's hands than like the hands of other teachers Charlotte had seen. Her dress was dark gray with narrow black ruching around the waist and neck. A small white shawl covered her broad shoulders and a white cap perched on her graying hair. Charlotte watched her as she read from a small worn Bible.

I will praise thee, O Lord, with my whole heart; I will shew forth all thy marvellous works.
I will be glad and rejoice in thee: I will sing praise to thy name, O thou most High.

Her voice was deep and mellow. The children listened mesmerized as the verse continued. What a remarkable teacher she was! She would have no trouble commanding the interest and respect of her students.

For the rest of the day Charlotte observed the classroom and worked with the younger students in a group where she listened to their recitations. After the children had left, Mercy Jackson suggested that she and Charlotte have tea and talk. They went into the small kitchen at the back of the building and sat down at a long, wooden table.

"Where did you hear about our school?" asked Mrs. Jackson as she poured tea into their cups, "Mr. Fox told me you had taught before but I understand that was not in New York."

"True enough, I have never been in New York before. I came here only a few days ago from Boston where I have been living ever since leaving England five years ago. In Massachusetts I taught at the Brook Farm School. You may have heard about it."

"Ah, yes indeed. Mr. Fox has spoken of that school with admiration. And we had a visitor a few months ago, the writer Margaret Fuller, who also mentioned the school. It is quite experimental I understand."

"All of us at the Brook Farm community were influenced by the teachings of Bronson Alcott. He taught us to listen to children as well as to lecture to them. Margaret Fuller admired his work although she did not always agree with his methods. It was she who recommended me to Mr. Fox when she heard he was looking for a teacher. Mr. Fox has told me that he strongly believes in Bronson Alcott's theories, as I suppose you do also."

Mercy Jackson looked out of the small kitchen window and then answered slowly, "I suppose I do believe in those theories, but to tell you the truth, the children we teach need so much help in such a short time that I scarcely think about theories. I am too busy trying to be sure the girls learn to read before they give up school. When winter comes hard, many will have to stay home because they don't have warm clothes. And whenever there is another baby in the family, they are kept home to help care for the infant. There are many obstacles to their education."

Charlotte had been raised in poverty in England but she expected life to be better in America. She wondered why the children were so poor. "Who pays for their schooling?"

Mercy turned her head to look closely at Charlotte. She sighed before she answered, "The school depends on the charity of a few wealthy men in the city. The families of most of the children would not be able to pay for tuition. Like me and my husband, many of them were slaves before they were given freedom by their former masters, sometimes individually and sometimes because a state decided to end slavery. But having freedom does not mean having the means to live. Freedom is almost as hard a road as being a slave was—although it is a road we will never give up." She frowned deeply as though threatening anyone who would take away her freedom.

"New York slaves were freed in 1827," she continued, "but my husband and I were given our freedom before that. We come from Virginia where we were owned by a wealthy man in Richmond. His wife had died before him and they never had children. In his will he gave freedom to all of his household slaves. More than that, he gave every one of us twenty dollars to start a new life.

"Being free blacks in Virginia was not easy. We could not walk down a road or ask for a job without being questioned about our master. We had to carry our papers everywhere. My husband James is a proud man and he was determined to live in a free state. We walked all the way up here from Virginia, and a long, weary trip it was. We travelled mostly by night because we were questioned so often if we were on the road during the day. Several times we had to stop in some town where James could work for money or for food. James is a skilled workman. Our master in Virginia had trained him to be a carpenter and to tune pianos. Many people need some carpentry work done, and sometimes a piano tuned.

"When we reached New York, we could breathe the air of freedom. James was able to find work as a piano tuner and we found a small place to stay. And like a gift from heaven I had a child. At last I had a child—the first one who lived. Always before my babies had died before their first year was up. But this one lived and thrived. We called him Freedom because he was born in 1827 in a free state."

"Is he still thriving?" Charlotte was almost afraid to ask.

"He's a beautiful young man now. Healthy as can be. He sings and dances like an angel and works almost every day. Freedom Jackson is a son to be proud of." Mercy Jackson's face shone as she talked about her son and her voice had a new lilt in it. Charlotte smiled as she heard that after so many hardships Mrs. Jackson and her husband had found solid happiness in their new city.

CHAPTER FOUR

Trouble on Thomas Street

Each separate dying ember wrought its ghost upon the floor.

Monday, November 13, 1843

By the time she got back to the boarding house, Charlotte was too late for dinner with the other boarders. The landlady insisted on serving the evening meal at exactly seven o'clock. Luckily for Charlotte, the cook had saved a meal for her and she was able to eat it in the kitchen. Daniel came in soon afterward and while Charlotte ate she told him about her day at school.

"Mrs. Jackson sounds like a remarkably strong woman," Daniel said. "It must have taken a lot of courage to travel so far with her husband. They were fortunate to have skills so they could find jobs here in the city."

Long after Charlotte went to bed that night she pondered what she had learned about the school where

35

she would be spending her days. If all of her pupils were poor, what would become of them? Were jobs so hard to find for free black families in New York? The questions were endless but Charlotte finally dropped off to sleep.

Her sleep was interrupted by a clanging bell in the street outside. It was still pitch black, but someone was shouting loudly although Charlotte could not make out what he was saying. Does this happen every night, she wondered, as she got out of bed. Are those young men attacking the brothel again? Haven't they anything better to do than to wake people in the middle of the night?

"Fire! Fire!" yelled a voice outside.

Charlotte ran toward the bedroom window. In the street men carrying lanterns were running toward the brothel. She couldn't see any flames, but a faint smell of smoke hung in the air.

The men on the fire truck ran into the house carrying buckets of water, but before long they came out again. The fire truck did not stay long; Charlotte saw the horses pull the heavy wagon down Thomas Street and around the corner. Only a night watchman was left in the street outside the door of the brothel. Charlotte could see figures carrying lanterns moving around inside the house. Then a few minutes later, someone arrived in a light buggy and entered the house. He carried a small bag—a doctor, Charlotte realized. She was tempted to go back to bed again but curiosity got the better of her.

Crouched by the window with her shawl clutched around her shoulders, Charlotte watched the people walking in and out of the house. Several men left rather quickly and hurried furtively away. They were customers, Charlotte realized, caught by accident in the very place they would be ashamed to mention to their wives or families.

Everything was quiet on the street for another several minutes. Then the door to the brothel opened wide and a small knot of silent men emerged. The doctor, clutching his small bag, was in the lead, with two watchmen following him. The doctor patted his horse on the flank and climbed up into the seat of the buggy. He exchanged a few words with the watchman and then flicked his whip over the horse. The buggy moved off.

Charlotte kept her eyes on the building while the watchman took up his place beside the door. She saw Mrs. Brown come out and attach a black knot of ribbon. What had happened? Was one of the women killed in the fire? Perhaps one of the two Charlotte had seen walking down Broadway so bright and free in their fancy dresses. What a sad end for such brilliant butterflies.

Several curious people walked up toward the house but the watchman blocked the doorway. A few men lingered outside, talking and arguing with the watchman, but they did not get very far. Eventually everything was quiet and Charlotte went back to bed.

The next morning, as Charlotte opened her eyes, the faint smell of smoke jolted her awake. She shivered remembering the fire alarm during the night. Activity at the house had started again. People walking by noticed the watchman and the black ribbon on the door. They gathered around the entrance and were soon rewarded by seeing a large dark carriage arrive. A man stepped out and entered the house as the gathering crowd surged closer. Soon the doctor's buggy returned and then two policemen joined the procession into the house. By the time Charlotte went down to breakfast no one in the boarding house could talk about anything except the excitement across the street.

Mrs. Richardson, who seemed to know most city officials by sight, told the boarders that the Chief of the Police Department was inside the brothel. He was conducting an inquiry she confidently told anyone who would listen. Most of the boarders crowded as close to the windows as they dared, shamelessly watching the commotion but not wanting to admit their curiosity.

Charlotte soon saw that Daniel had joined the group in the street and was busily trying to note down what people were saying. She would have liked to join him, but it was scarcely possible for a respectable woman to be part of such a crowd. Eventually the policeman came to the door and selected a group of men from the crowd, seemingly choosing anyone who volunteered.

"They will serve as the coroner's jury," Mrs. Richardson told the women in the boarding house. "That is exactly how it was done when poor Mrs. Smith died so suddenly after falling down the back steps of her house. They need to decide the cause of death. I daresay if a young woman was burned to death the cause is easy to see."

Whatever the coroner's jury decided, Charlotte would not learn about it until that evening. She had to hurry off to school to meet her classes.

The stumbling young man who had been struggling to teach the boys had decided that working for his father's business was easier than teaching, so he was leaving the school. John Fox planned to divide the pupils into three classes—one for the youngest children who knew nothing of reading, and the other two for older students who were wrestling with longer words and more difficult stories. Charlotte was given the youngest class of boys and girls while Mercy Jackson taught the older girls and John Fox took the boys. Charlotte was busy all morning helping her primary students get used to being in school. She found they were eager to learn and delighted in the Mother Goose songs she taught them.

By the time school was over Charlotte felt tired but satisfied with her work. As she walked back to the boarding house, she heard the sound of voices in the parlor. The parlor door opened and a woman in a brilliant green dress stepped out into the hall. Charlotte recognized her as one of the two women she had seen walking on Broadway the first day she had arrived in the city. She was still talking to someone in the room behind her.

"I can assure you I will cause you no trouble or difficulty. After what happened to poor Susan last night, I have no intention of leading a gay life for some time to come." When she saw Charlotte in the hallway, she turned and said. "My name is Rowena Scott. Mrs. Richardson has just told me that I can rent a room in this house for a week or so. My rooms were destroyed by the terrible fire last night. Perhaps you saw it?"

"Yes, indeed," responded Charlotte. "I am glad you escaped safely. My name is Charlotte Edgerton and I have only been living in the city for a few days. The fire was a dreadful shock. We could hardly be unaware of it and were glad to see that the firemen and watchmen came to put it out quickly. I could see there was someone injured in the fire."

"That was my friend Susan Jones. I regret to tell you that she died in the fire."

"I am very sorry to hear that. How did the fire start? Did someone overturn a lamp?"

"It was much worse than that. I am afraid that someone deliberately set fire to Susan's bed. The sheriff has told us that she had probably died before that happened."

"How horrible!" cried Charlotte. "Who could have done such a thing?"

"Who indeed? Susan had many friends. She had clients who were very fond of her. One of them in particular, Lawrence Abingdon, often showed her his poetry and read it to her. Indeed he often read his poems to all of us. Have you ever heard any of them? Oh, I cannot bear to think we will never spend another evening listening to him read." She lifted her handkerchief to her eyes and bowed her head.

The silence passed and Rowena soon continued. "Mr. Abingdon's poems tell beautiful tales of lovely ladies in castles and of the knights who rescue them from danger. Susan was extremely fond of his poetry and so am I.

> *In the greenest of our valleys*
>   *By good angels tenanted,*
> *Once a fair and stately palace-*
>   *Radiant palace- reared its head.*
> *In the monarch Thought's dominion-*
>   *It stood there!*
> *Never seraph spread a pinion*
>   *Over fabric half so fair!"*

As she recited the poem, Rowena's eyes filled with tears that finally spilled over and crept down her cheeks. "That was one of Susan's favorites. Mr. Abingdon recited it many times."

"You must have so many memories of Miss Jones. It will no doubt be painful for you to return to that house," said Charlotte. "I am glad you will be staying here for a while."

Charlotte wondered whether Mrs. Richardson was aware of Rowena's profession. In the boarding house there were many rules about the behavior of boarders. No gentlemen were allowed in any room except the parlor, and their visits must end by ten o'clock at night.

Mrs. Richardson was a stickler for respectability. She would never allow her house to be confused with a brothel.

The dinner gong rang, so the two women went into the dining room and sat down at the table with the others. Rowena was introduced, but the boarders had little to say to her. Charlotte noticed the quiet widowed seamstress who lived on the second floor with her young son glanced often at Rowena's dress, which certainly was a sharp contrast to the dull gray and black dresses of the other boarders. Rowena was the only one at the table who attempted conversation and her remarks were limited to weather and the possibility of rain. Charlotte smiled thinking the remarks might be dull but they were certainly respectable.

After the meal was finished, Charlotte went into the parlor to wait for Daniel. Rowena trailed after her and chose a chair close to Charlotte's.

"Have you lived in New York very long?" she asked. When she heard that Charlotte was a newcomer, she offered herself as a guide.

"I have lived here for almost five years now," she told Charlotte. "I grew up in Maine, but life in the country is too quiet for me so I was happy to get away to the big city."

"Did you come to find work?"

"Yes, I thought I could be a seamstress and indeed I worked in a dressmaking shop for a while. But the pay is miserable, you know, and the working hours are very long. I am a girl who loves parties and fun. Losing my eyesight poring over needlework was no life for me. Mrs. Brown used to come into the shop to buy dresses. Oh, what lovely dresses she bought! She had so many of them and so many gentlemen friends who bought her gloves or hats. She introduced me to some of them and I soon found there was much better work than struggling in a dress shop." She smoothed the bright green skirt of her dress and smiled at Charlotte mischievously.

Just then Daniel arrived. Charlotte introduced him to Rowena, who remembered him from his visit to the brothel a few days before. "And will you come and pay us another visit when the fire damage has been repaired?" she asked him with a friendly smile.

Daniel frowned and Charlotte thought she saw him blush. His reply was rather stiff. "I am investigating the fire and the death of Susan Jones for my newspaper the *Tribune.* My only interest in Mrs. Brown's establishment, I assure you, is in discovering the villain who committed the crime."

"Have you learned anything more about what happened?" Charlotte asked.

"The doctor thinks the woman was strangled before her bed was set on fire. Evidently the killer thought the body would be destroyed in the flames and his crime would not be discovered. Now the question is: where did he go? How did he escape?"

"Does the sheriff have any idea?" asked Charlotte. "Who was in the house?" She turned to Rowena.

"I do not know who might have been visiting the house that night," said Rowena, drawing herself up forbiddingly. "I do not keep watch on my friends. Any woman can have a visitor if she wishes. Sometimes Mrs. Brown lets them in and sometimes her husband or one of the women will do that. The door is locked at midnight, but some guests stay overnight."

"Was Lawrence Abingdon one of the visitors last night?" asked Daniel. "There seems to be some suspicion that he was."

"Well, yes," Rowena admitted. "I did see him briefly early in the evening. He played a piece on the piano for us and Susan sang. What was the song? Oh, I remember. It was "Come Where My Love Lies Dreaming". What a beautiful song that is."

"The sheriff's men are interested in finding out how long Mr. Abingdon stayed. No one seems to know. Or at least they say they don't know. Mrs. Brown was quite indignant about being asked about it." Daniel frowned as he spoke.

"What time was the fire?" asked Charlotte. "It was after midnight surely. And if the door was locked at midnight, couldn't all of the people in the house be accounted for?"

"There was a great scattering when the fire alarms sounded," admitted Rowena. "Several men ran out of the house in a panic, although there was no danger. The fire was a small one. It was only smoldering when Mrs.

Brown discovered it. She and I could have put it out ourselves."

"Where was Mr. Brown while all this was going on?" Charlotte was curious about who was in charge. Everyone talked as though Mrs. Brown was, but surely her husband must play a role.

Rowena tossed her head scornfully. "Mr. Brown rarely spends the evening—or the night—at home. He is very fond of a tavern down on Broadway and spends most of his evenings there only coming home late in the morning."

"So you have no idea who might have been in the house visiting Susan Jones that night?" asked Daniel. "How could anyone leave if the door was locked?"

"The back door is not locked so securely at night," Rowena said. "People sometimes need to go into the back yard to the outhouse. There is a high fence around the yard so there is no need to keep the door securely locked. In fact, Mrs. Brown and I noticed that it was open last night."

"That must have been how the killer escaped," exclaimed Charlotte. "Wouldn't it be possible for someone to climb over a fence if he was very frightened of being caught? The neighbors would likely be asleep and wouldn't notice him."

Daniel was on his feet now and striding up and down across the parlor. "That's what the sheriff thinks. And it seems they suspect Mr. Abingdon of doing just that. I believe they are searching for him now and intend to arrest him for murder."

"Oh no! It could not have been Lawrence Abingdon," insisted Rowena. "He would not have hurt Susan. He was very fond of her. I will go to the police. I will plead with the court. They are making a terrible mistake. There were others in the house. Someone else must be responsible—not Lawrence Abingdon."

CHAPTER FIVE

Changing New York City

Ye of the coarser sex who often rave
At fallen women, but never try to save;
Inform me, tell me, if you can,
What art thou but a fallen man?

Wednesday, November 15, 1843

On Wednesday as Charlotte approached the school, she saw children clustered around the door; they greeted her with bright smiles. When she led them into the classroom, they settled on to their long benches and waited while she handed each one of them a small slate. Thanks to the generosity of the school's Board of Trustees, each child now had his or her own slate instead of having to share with others. Charlotte started reading the alphabet rhyme to them "A is for apple" and then showed them how to draw each letter.

Despite some squabbling over who had broken Willie Green's chalk and giggles over how difficult it was to remember the difference between a 'b' and a 'd' they somehow got through the morning. When the lunch break time came, Charlotte and Mercy sat at the kitchen table to eat the dinners they had brought with them. No sooner had they sat down when the door opened and an African man came in.

"This is my husband, James Jackson", Mercy introduced him to Charlotte. "What are you doing here so early in the day?"

Mr. Jackson was a tall, thin man with graying hair and expressive brown eyes. His smile showed a row of very white teeth as he bowed his head toward Charlotte. "I am very pleased to meet you Miss Edgerton. I hope you will enjoy teaching at this school. My wife tells me you have had experience at a fine school in Massachusetts."

After they had talked about school for a few minutes, Mr. Jackson explained why he had come so early. "Mr. Rex Hamilton, a trustee here at the school, is giving a speech this afternoon at the plaza in front of City Hall. He asked me to pick up the placards at the school and meet him at City Hall. I will hand out placards and take care of lighting for the event. Our son Freedom is also going be there. He will entertain the crowd with some songs and dances before Mr. Hamilton's speech begins. Perhaps you would enjoy hearing the speech, Miss Edgerton?"

Charlotte was certainly interested in hearing the speech and also in seeing Freedom Jackson who was, according to his mother, a talented dancer and musician.

When the time came she walked the short distance to City Hall with Mr. and Mrs. Jackson. They all carried signs proclaiming "Rex Hamilton for Mayor".

A makeshift platform had been set up in the plaza to make the speaker more visible. A crowd was already gathering around the platform watching the entertainment. On stage a slight young African boy was doing a lively step-dance that reminded Charlotte of the Irish dances her friend Ellen used to do. This must be Freedom Jackson. Charlotte could see why his mother had said he was talented. His feet moved quickly on the floor and tapped out a lively rhythm that made her want to join in the dancing. When he stopped, he took a harmonica out of his pocket and played a familiar tune. "O Bowery Gals won't you come out tonight?" Many of the men and women watching the performance sang along with the music.

Then it was time for the speech to begin. Two chairs were placed on the stage and soon Rex Hamilton and John Fox appeared and settled into them. John Fox started the proceedings by explaining that the theme of the program was "Saving the City from Sin and Corruption". He did not speak very long but introduced Rex Hamilton who, he said, was a leading businessman, a guardian of public morals, and "soon to be the mayor of this great city". When he said those words, James Jackson led a cheer and applause and several men in the audience joined in.

Rex Hamilton began his talk by calling upon all citizens to unite to save the city of New York from the sin and corruption into which it had fallen. "Our streets are cesspools where prostitution, gambling and other sinful pursuits are openly carried on. Our police and public officials ignore this sinful behavior and allow it to flourish. I say to you we have become the Sodom and Gomorrah of America. I have heard it said that from Boston to Charleston our great city, New York, is known as Sin City. Is this the kind of city you want to live in? Let me hear you say it!"

Slowly a few people in the crowd shouted "No...no" and then more voices joined in. Charlotte was impressed with how Rex Hamilton had roused the crowd. She looked around and saw more and more of the men smiling and cheering. She also saw a familiar figure near the side of the crowd and moved toward him.

Daniel had his usual notebook in front of him and was noting down what Rex Hamilton was saying. He turned when he realized Charlotte was there. "What are you doing at this rally?" he asked. "I am covering it for my newspaper. Why are you here? I would have thought you would be too tired to join the crowd."

"Rex Hamilton is one of the trustees of the Pearl Street School. And the man who introduced him is John Fox, the master of the school. Come with me and I will introduce you to Mrs. Jackson, who teaches with me, and her husband. It is their son, Freedom, who performed the dance and played the harmonica earlier."

Rex Hamilton continued talking, although the crowd was becoming restless. People moved about and stopped to talk with friends only half listening to the speaker. Charlotte quickly introduced Daniel to the Jacksons and the four of them watched the crowd and the speaker. Dark was falling and James Jackson and another man placed torches around the stage. Soon a garish reddish light flickered on Rex Hamilton's face as he spoke.

"We must put an end to the brothels that fill our streets and corrupt our young men," he was saying. "New York is filled with innocent farm boys coming to the city to earn a living, but many are ruined by the painted women who entice them into places of sin. Women who flaunt their shining dresses and sparkling jewels. Their clothes are worth more than an honest man can make in a year. Should we allow this to continue?"

"No, no" shouted voices from the crowd. A man standing near Charlotte turned to his neighbor and laughed grimly, "Time for another spree, do you think?" He grinned as he said it and Charlotte shuddered as she remembered the men who had attacked the brothel on Thomas Street.

Rex Hamilton was continuing his speech. "We must destroy these brothels! We must close disorderly taverns!"

"Yes, yes," shouted the crowd and about twenty men started moving out of the plaza and toward the downtown streets.

"I do not ask you to turn to violence," said Rex Hamilton quickly. "We will do these things lawfully," but his voice was lost as the crowd broke up and many of the men moved off laughing and calling to one another.

"Time for a brawl, brothers" Charlotte heard someone shout.

"We must get the women out of here," Mr. Jackson said to Daniel. "There is going to be trouble tonight."

Charlotte swung her arms angrily as she walked back to the boarding house with Daniel. "Rex Hamilton says he is only interested in cleaning up the city—making it more 'pure' as he says, but encouraging attacks on defenseless women doesn't seem right to me."

"He's right about corruption in the city though," Daniel insisted. "When I visited that brothel the other day, Mayor Simpson was there friendly as he could be. It's not illegal to run a brothel, but I'm not too happy about what goes on there. Some of the girls were very young. One of them reminded me of my sister, and I wouldn't want to see her sitting on some old man's lap."

"Rowena Scott seems happy enough," Charlotte reminded him. "But of course she's old enough to know her own mind. How young are the girls there? Where do they come from?"

"Most of them come to the city from upstate New York or New England. Some of them are immigrants, I'm sure. Everyone thinks there are plenty of jobs in the city, but jobs aren't easy to find especially for someone who is an immigrant and doesn't have friends in the city. A lot of people don't give jobs to the Irish. And even if a person finds a job, the pay often isn't enough to live on."

"Where will the women go if Hamilton becomes mayor and shuts down the brothels? Some of them will be out on the street and that's worse than a brothel." Charlotte could remember seeing young girls in England walking the streets of Southampton looking for men who would give them someplace to stay for the night. She hadn't thought she'd see the same thing in America.

By this time they had reached the boarding house. "I'm going to go back to the meeting and see whether any of the men there are planning to attack a brothel tonight. I'll let you know tomorrow what I find out. But let's talk about something else. I've been waiting so long for you to get here and thinking about things we can do. But you've seen nothing but trouble ever since you arrived. Sure we both deserve some good times. Perhaps on Saturday I could take you to the theater to see something entertaining. We can ask Eileen to come along if she can get the evening off."

"That would be wonderful. I've never been to a real theater."

"There's only one thing we need to do. I have to tell Eileen about the plan and there isn't time to write a note. Do you think you could walk over to the Van Pelt house tomorrow after school and ask her whether she could meet us on Saturday? They live in Washington Square not far from your school."

"Of course I will. I'd like to see the Van Pelt mansion. From the way Eileen described it, there will be a lot to see. She said the furniture was all imported from England and the draperies were made in France. It must be a very luxurious house."

"I'm not sure how much of the house you'll see. That depends on who is home, but at least you'll have a glimpse of it."

CHAPTER SIX

Seeing How Others Live

In truth I have wandered this wide world over
Yet Ireland's my home and a dwelling for me.

Friday, November 17, 1843

The next morning Charlotte found a worried Mercy Jackson at the school.

"There was another spree last night," she said grimly. "Men left Mr. Hamilton's speech and went right off to attack a sporting house near City Hall. My husband saw them yelling and running away."

"Was anyone hurt?" Charlotte remembered how brutal some of the men had looked.

"There is no way to tell yet. I suppose the newspapers will have reports later today. What is happening to cause all this violence in the city?"

When the afternoon classes were over, Charlotte walked to Washington Square and found the Van Pelt mansion, a large, brownstone house with wide windows. She was tempted to walk up the broad stoop and knock on the elaborate front door, but she knew she would be expected to go down the side steps to the servant's area below. Americans might think of themselves as very democratic, but they expected servants to behave like English servants. At the back door, Charlotte knocked and a footman admitted her to a low-ceilinged room just below ground level. The windows looked out on the front yard and the street beyond. Eileen Gallagher soon appeared and led her back to the kitchen where they could talk.

"Your brother wants to take you and me to the theater on Saturday night to see a play called *Beauty and the Beast.* Charlotte was excited to share the news and Eileen received it enthusiastically. Both of them had heard about the plays at the new Park Theater but neither had ever seen one.

"I'll have to wear my Sunday dress," said Eileen. "And I should try to find a ribbon to make my bonnet fancier. My yellow flower was ruined in the rain. Come upstairs and I'll show you. Maybe you can give me some ideas. Cook won't be giving me work for an hour or so when we start setting the table."

The back stairs of the house were dark and bare. On the top floor they opened onto a narrow hallway and Eileen led the way to her room. It was barely large enough for the two maids who shared it. Eileen had two hooks for her dresses—one for her uniform and one for her Sunday dress. Her undergarments were in a flat box kept under the bed.

Eileen brought out her bonnet and showed Charlotte the bedraggled yellow flower that was its only trimming. Charlotte helped her to take the flower off the hat and offered to bring Eileen some bright blue ribbon left over from trimming her own bonnet. By this time Eileen seemed like an old friend.

"Do you think I could look at some of the rooms in the house?" Charlotte asked. "The furniture must be beautiful and I would love to see it."

Soon enough they were downstairs tip-toeing down the hallway toward the front parlor. Eileen was about to open the door when someone inside pulled it open and two men came out. One of them Charlotte recognized as Rex Hamilton, the other was an older man with white hair who walked rather slowly leaning on a cane. Neither of them paid the slightest attention to Eileen in her maid's uniform or to Charlotte standing behind her. They walked across the hall to the library talking steadily all the time.

"I am one of the trustees at the Pearl Street School," Rex Hamilton was explaining. "I don't object to educating our black brethren and it goes over well with many of our voters, especially Quakers and reformers. Of course, it's a joke—you can't expect those darkies to learn much…" His voice trailed off as the two men entered the library and closed the door.

"That was Rex Hamilton, wasn't it? The man who wants to become Mayor of New York? What is he doing here? He isn't talking the way he talked when he visited the school. He talked a lot about how important education was for the free blacks." Charlotte was shocked.

"Indeed it is Rex Hamilton. He is married to Maria Van Pelt, the oldest Van Pelt daughter. He often comes here, especially when his wife is in the country for her health. I didn't know you knew him."

"Well, as you heard, Rex Hamilton is a trustee at the school where I teach. Several of us from the school went to hear him speak last night and I found out he was running for Mayor of New York. I was surprised to meet your brother there, but of course he has to follow the politics of the city."

"You don't sound as though you like the idea of Mr. Hamilton becoming the mayor."

"Last night he talked a great deal about making the city 'pure' and I am afraid he roused some of the men to attack a brothel and cause damage. I don't like to see women being attacked no matter how they make a living. Many women have no choice except to work in a brothel. Jobs are hard to find and people have to eat."

"I don't know anything about that," Eileen didn't seem too interested in politics. "Mr. Hamilton visits the house often, but he has never paid any special attention to me.

He's not like young Mr. Charles Van Pelt who always has a cheerful word for me." Eileen smiled dreamily. "And for any of the other staff," she added hastily.

Saturday came quickly. Charlotte was glad to catch up on her chores and get ready for the trip to the theater. Eileen joined her at the boarding house and Charlotte gave her the ribbon and helped her trim her bonnet. Daniel arrived soon after to escort the women to the theater.

"Have you discovered anything more about who killed Susan Jones?" Charlotte asked him. "Are the police still looking for Lawrence Abingdon?"

"They are looking, but there are very few police in the city. I don't know what they can do to find a man who wants to remain hidden. If he valued his good name, he would come forward and talk to the police. This hiding away makes him seem guilty." Daniel frowned with disapproval.

The evening was chilly with a harsh wind blowing down Broadway as they turned the corner. A crowd of people hovered around the entrance to the grand theater.

Their seats were in a box at the side of the theater where they could easily see the audience. Despite the darkness outside, the theater was bright. Candelabra were placed at intervals around the sides of the theater and gas lights illuminated the stage. Men were filling the ground floor, coming into the building in pairs and groups, smoking cigars and talking. Couples and families sat comfortably in the boxes; women in silk dresses, with shawls and cloaks of velvet or wool and elaborate fans, looked around and nodded to friends in other boxes. The balcony above the boxes was shadowy, but Charlotte could see that the seats were filled mostly with women chatting with one another or with the men who moved around the aisles talking with them. This was the famous "third tier," the only section where women without escorts were allowed to sit. Up there, Daniel had told her, prostitutes were free to meet men and make arrangements to see them after the show. Some of the respectable husbands who took their wives to the boxes were said to haunt the third tier to make assignations with sporting girls for an after-hours encounter. This was a far cry from the austere public gatherings Charlotte had seen in Massachusetts. She knew prostitution existed everywhere, even in Boston, but it was scarcely visible there and certainly not flaunted the way it was in New York.

When the play started, attention shifted to the stage, but it was difficult not to be distracted by action in the audience. Charlotte would have been happier if the theater lights had been dimmed, but they burned brightly and many people in the theater carried on their conversations and flirtations as actively as they had before the performance started.

Charlotte tried to fix her attention on the stage. The actor playing the Beast seemed to be borrowing words from Shakespeare as he stomped across the stage. He tried to tell the frightened Beauty about the kingdom where he lived, using the words of Caliban:

Be not afeard; the isle is full of noises,
Sounds, and sweet airs, that give delight and hurt not.
Sometimes a thousand twangling instruments
Will hum about mine ears; and sometime voices
That, if I then had waked after long sleep,
Will make me sleep again; and then in dreaming,
The clouds methought would open, and show riches
Ready to drop upon me, that when I waked
I cried to dream again.

Actors had to reuse speeches once they had learned them otherwise they would never get through all the plays they were expected to perform. Was the ungainly Beast on the stage really a Shakespearean actor at heart? But Charlotte's thoughts were interrupted by Daniel's urgent whisper.

"Look above! There is our friend Rowena Scott in the upper balcony. Who is the man she is talking with? I do believe it is Lawrence Abingdon. With the police in the city looking for him how can he dare show himself in a theater?"

Charlotte looked up and could clearly see Rowena in her bright green dress. She was talking with a young man in a dark suit who leaned toward her protectively. Even as she watched the two of them she saw a disturbance start in the balcony. Two men were approaching the pair.

There was a loud shout as Lawrence Abingdon's arm was seized by one of the men. "Let me go! What do you want of me?"

For a moment the action stopped on stage as both actors and audience turned to stare up at the balcony. The two burly policemen pulled Abingdon to his feet and led him toward the balcony stairs. "Shame! Shame!" came some cries from the audience. Other men applauded and urged the policemen on. Rowena was following them and someone called out to her, "Leave the police alone, you hussy".

But soon it was all over. The actors remembered where they were and the play resumed. Charlotte was unable to concentrate on what was happening onstage. The police thought Susan's killer had been taken into custody, but Charlotte was not convinced the right man had been arrested.

When the play was over, Daniel and the two women moved slowly out of the crowded theater. The crowd was in a festive mood and streamed noisily down Broadway.

"Would you two young ladies care to stop at an oyster bar for a cool drink and a bite to eat?"

"Oh, Daniel, will you take me back to that lively place we went to when I first arrived?" Eileen asked quickly. "The one with all the Irish singers and the oysterman who comes from Cork?"

They soon joined the crowd pushing toward O'Donnell's Oyster House and found themselves seats near the wall. Three steins full of beer appeared on their table as Daniel went up to the bar to supervise the shucking of their oysters. Charlotte saw him pause to greet several men. Soon he was back with a wooden bowl full of oysters.

Someone at the bar started singing a melancholy song. Most of the audience, including Daniel and Eileen joined in the chorus:

> In truth I have wandered this wide world over,
> Yet Ireland's my home and a dwelling for me.
> And, oh, let the turf that my old bones shall cover
> Be cut from the land that is trod by the free.

Soon almost everyone in the place was singing and shouting. Tears streamed down the cheeks of some of the women, and a few of the men. A tall burly man moved to the center of the room and started singing:

> A nation once again
> A nation once again
> And Ireland long a province be
> A nation once again.

Daniel jumped from his seat and stood at the man's side, joining him in singing. Charlotte watched him thinking he looked younger joining in this crowd whose experiences and backgrounds were so much like his own. His cheeks were flushed and a lock of his dark hair slipped over his pale forehead.

"Let's drink a toast to Ireland," shouted one man, "May she soon be freed of her chains."

"Ireland, land of our birth," called another man lifting his glass. Almost everyone stood up and lifted their glasses.

When they had finished their toast, Daniel lifted his glass again, "And here's to America and the freedom it gives us! May our two homelands always live in peace."

The singing and drinking seemed to go on forever. By the time they left the oyster bar, Charlotte was worn out. She had seen more of New York this evening than she ever had before. And more of Daniel too. Like him she knew that she would always have two homelands.

CHAPTER SEVEN

Daniel Visits the Tombs

My limbs are bowed, though not with toil,
But rusted with a vile repose,
For they have been a dungeon's spoil.

Sunday, November 19, 1843

After seeing Lawrence Abingdon arrested Saturday
evening, Daniel decided to visit the jail early on Sunday
and see what was going on. Did the police have any
evidence against Abingdon? Were they just suspicious
only because he had visited Susan so often? Was it
possible that Abingdon was the killer?

As Daniel approached the Halls of Justice, more often
called the "Tombs", he could see the gray walls looming
over an entire city block. Some people said the building
was a beautiful example of fine architecture, but Daniel
thought Charles Dickens had a more sensible view. He
had asked when he saw it, "What is this dismal fronted

pile of bastard Egyptian, like an enchanter's palace in a melodrama?" Dickens had it right.

The guards appeared relaxed so early in the morning and the holding room was quiet. One prisoner slumped on the floor in a drunken sleep, while another looked up at Daniel and muttered hopelessly that he was hungry and needed to get home to his wife.

"I am a reporter for the *Tribune*," Daniel told the presiding guard. "I would like to speak to Lawrence Abingdon, the man you arrested at the theater last night."

"A reporter, are you?" the guard asked and Daniel smiled as he recognized the accent of his native Galway. "Sure, there's not many of us have reached that high. But is it really the murderer you want to see? He's the most popular prisoner we've had in a long time. There was a charming young lady—well, I wouldn't call her a lady— but she was a woman who argued like a judge about getting 'Poor Mr. Abingdon' out of prison. She said he never would have been so brutal as to have killed her friend. We paid no attention of course. It stands to reason that he's guilty."

"How can you be so sure? Is there any proof he did it?"

"He admits to having visited the woman. To read his poetry he says. A likely story that is! No one saw anyone else enter her room and Mr. Abingdon disappeared from the house like a leprechaun with a pot of gold."

"I would like to speak with him," Daniel persisted. "Our readers will want to know what he has to say for himself."

Daniel was let into the cell where Lawrence Abingdon was being held. He looked very different from the confident man Daniel had seen reciting poetry the week before. He sat on a small cot, holding his head in his hands. As he lifted his head his face was ashen and his unshaven cheeks sprouted black stubble. He looked the image of despair.

When Daniel entered the cell, Abingdon sprang to his feet quickly and looked at him eagerly. "Who are you? Is there any news? Do the police realize their mistake?"

"My name is Daniel Gallagher and I represent the *Tribune* newspaper. I want to let the public know about your case. The police tell me you visited the dead woman the night she died. How was she when you saw her?"

"She was happy and healthy, a perfectly contented young woman when I left. The police suggested we might have quarreled, but we had no quarrel. I read her a new poem and she was happy to hear it. I have high hopes of having it published soon."

"But why did no one see you leave?"

"That I cannot say, Mr. Gallagher. I am a rather quiet fellow. Perhaps no one was paying attention."

"You must have known the police were looking for you these last few days. Would it not have been better to inform them of your whereabouts and cleared this matter up? Sure, everyone in the city, including myself, thought you had fled. That is until I saw you at the theater last night talking with Miss Scott. I understand she was here to see you this morning. Is she a good friend of yours?"

"She proved herself a good friend this morning, Mr. Gallagher. She told the police that I would not have harmed a hair on the head of any woman, especially not Susan Jones. And she was right. I am a poet, not a violent man who attacks women."

"Did the police believe Miss Scott?"

"I am afraid they rather laughed at her. She grew quite shrill in my defense and even lapsed into French, but that did nothing to move the hearts of the officers."

Daniel was puzzled to hear that Rowena Scott would "lapse into French" when she was excited. Surely she had not had the kind of education that would give her a mastery of other languages. Was there some secret about her that he and Charlotte had not heard? But he had no time to think about that.

Daniel had questions he wanted to ask Lawrence Abingdon, but the policeman came back to the cell and told him to leave. "You've had plenty of time to interview the prisoner, young man. Now when you write this up for your newspaper I hope you'll tell people what good care we are taking of him. We have found the vicious killer without wasting time. Now the streets of the city are safe again."

Daniel smiled grimly as he left. He had no plan to tell people how efficient the new policemen were, although he was glad that New York was at last getting itself a force that could handle the growing crime in the city. He walked back to Charlotte's boarding house thinking that the police were too well satisfied. Lawrence might be the man who had strangled Susan Jones and set fire to her, but his talk and actions were not those of a guilty killer.

Daniel had known a man back in Ireland who had seemed peaceable enough but had nonetheless killed his landlord when he was thrown off his piece of land. But killing a landlord in a fit of anger is nothing like deliberately killing a young woman to whom you have been so close. Was it jealousy? But who would Lawrence be jealous of? Susan was not his wife. He had no claim on her. And no matter how much Daniel tried to imagine the scene, he could not picture the pale young poet violently attacking a young woman.

Charlotte was waiting for Daniel, who found to his surprise that she had a visitor. Rowena Scott was sitting in the parlor and so was Mrs. Brown, the owner of the brothel. This was surely the first time Charlotte had been in such company, but she seemed quite at home with the two women. They were all glad to see Daniel and to hear what he had learned at the prison. Rowena had already told them about her failure to convince the police they had made a mistake.

"They have no thought of mistakes," Daniel told them. "In fact, they seem very satisfied with their work. The man in charge wants me to write a story pointing out what a good job the police are doing in taking care of the city."

"What do you think?" Charlotte asked quietly. "Do you think Mr. Abingdon is guilty?"

"Guilty he cannot be!" exclaimed Rowena excitedly. "He is a man of deep feeling who writes beautiful poetry. How could he do such a monstrous thing? It is impossible!" As she spoke, it sounded to Daniel as though she might break into French at any minute. This was the first time he had noticed her slight accent.

"Do you speak French, Miss Scott?" he asked curiously.

"Yes, yes. When I am excited I cannot help going back to my mother tongue. I will confess to you. I was not born with the name Rowena Scott, although that is the name I choose to use. It is such a beautiful name. I learned to love the novels of Sir Walter Scott and even more to love his beautiful heroine Rowena. When I came to New York it was to get away from my old life and to build a new one where I could live like a lovely Scott heroine."

"Are you from France then?" Charlotte asked, but got a frown instead of an answer.

"Oh, I shall not bore you with my life story. I am Rowena Scott from Quebec and that is how you know me. If I burst into French sometimes it is only because part of my soul lives in French and always will. But in New York I am just another American girl."

Daniel turned his attention to Mrs. Brown. "Perhaps it is true that Lawrence did not hurt Susan, but if he is not guilty the police will be looking for another suspect. Who else was at your house last night?"

Even as he said it, Daniel realized what a sensitive issue he had raised. Most of the men who had visited would not want their names identified, especially if they were prominent citizens like the Mayor. Was there any way to find out who frequented the brothel?

Mrs. Brown looked for a moment as though she would not answer, but then she reconsidered. "We had quite a little gathering in the parlor as we often do. You were there yourself last week if I remember rightly, Mr. Gallagher."

Daniel nodded his head briefly in agreement.

"As you know I have a fine piano and several of the young ladies are excellent musicians. We often have music in the evening. But the piano, I am afraid, was getting somewhat out of tune. On the particular night you mention, I had our piano tuner come to service it. He was there quite late into the evening because he had to replace a key which had been broken."

"And who is it who tunes your piano?"

"His name is James Jackson and he is an excellent workman. He was trained in the South I believe and is considered the most competent piano tuner in the city."

"That must be Mercy Jackson's husband," interrupted Charlotte. "She told me her husband had learned how to tune pianos while he was still a slave in Virginia."

"But he would have been working in the parlor," Daniel remarked. "And he would not likely have stayed after the music was finished. I do not see how he could be implicated in any of the trouble."

Mrs. Brown frowned while he spoke, finally she jumped in. "I know that Mr. Jackson is a good piano tuner, but I have always been afraid of him. He smiles too much. And he is so black. If he were a good man, God would have made him white like us."

"What are you saying?" Charlotte interrupted. "Do you really think you can judge by the color of his skin? Mrs. Jackson is one of the teachers at my school and she is certainly a good person. I think her husband is too."

Mrs. Brown swept to her feet. "You are entitled to your opinions, but you will find many people agree with me. Mr. Abingdon is a gentleman. He is not a killer. It must be this man Jackson who was consumed by jealously for a pretty white girl. You will see that Mr. Abingdon will be cleared of the murder and Mr. Jackson will prove to be evil."

The room was silent while Mrs. Brown and Rowena Scott rose, put on their coats and left.

CHAPTER EIGHT

More Questions but Few Answers

-- 'You left us in tatters, without shoes or socks,
Tired of digging potatoes, and spudding up docks;
And now you've gay bracelets and bright feathers three!' –
'Yes: that's how we dress when we're ruined,' said she.

Friday, November 24, 1843

For the rest of that week Charlotte taught her classes,
shared her lunch hour with Mercy Jackson, and prepared
lessons as usual, but she felt confused and unsettled. She
knew some people were frightened of black people and
distrusted them, but she had never heard that feeling
expressed so vehemently before. As she looked at the
children in her class she wondered how other people saw
them. Would their skin color be seen as a mark against
them? The words that Mrs. Brown had said about James
Jackson echoed in her ears every time she looked at
Mercy Jackson. Would the police feel the way Mrs.
Brown did?

73

One morning she led the children in a recitation of a favorite poem:

Little Lamb who made thee
Dost thou know who made thee?
Gave thee life & bid thee feed.
By the stream & o'er the mead;
Gave thee clothing of delight,
Softest clothing wooly bright;
Gave thee such a tender voice,
Making all the vales rejoice!
Little Lamb who made thee
Dost thou know who made thee?

Did anyone really believe the small children who stood in front of her could be anything but innocent? Charlotte remembered Bronson Alcott and the faith he had that all children had goodness in them. Why would one of them grow up to become a killer? Of course, whoever killed Susan must have been a child once. It was all too much to think about. She had never met Lawrence Abingdon and had no reason to think he was either good or bad, but someone had done this terrible thing.

Daniel came over every evening and shared with her the news of the day. He had written a story about Susan Jones for his newspaper and he showed her the paper.

The cold-blooded and heartless murder of a young woman who was a familiar figure on the streets of New York has aroused the public as few other crimes in recent years have done. Is this a city where such evil deeds go unpunished? Now at last it appears that someone has been arrested for the crime.

The police have not explained what proof they have linking the accused to the crime. They have ignored requests from reporters for information about why they made this arrest. The facts are most unusual. Lawrence Abingdon is not one of the hooligans who make our streets unsafe. Quite the contrary. He is the son of a leading family in Richmond, Virginia, and has been widely acknowledged as one of the rising young poets of our day. Witness these lines he penned just a few short months ago:

Like music heard in dreams,
Like strains of harps unknown,
Of birds for ever flown,
— Audible as the voice of streams
That murmur in some leafy dell,
I hear thy gentlest tone,
And Silence cometh with her spell
Like that which on my tongue doth dwell,
When tremulous in dreams I tell
My love to thee alone!

Is the author of these lines truly the man who committed the hideous murder of which he is accused? The people of New York will not be satisfied until the secret of this crime is unraveled and we hear from the guilty man's lips the true story of what happened that dreadful night.

"Have you heard of any proof that Lawrence Abingdon committed the crime?" Charlotte asked Daniel every evening. "Are the police still investigating? Still trying to discover something that connects him with Susan's death? If he keeps insisting he did not kill her and they have no definite proof, how can they keep him in jail?"

Daniel had spent hours at the jail and the Halls of Justice trying to answer that question. "They say that a note in his hand was found in the bedroom underneath some of her clothes in a drawer. Although they have not released the note, I have heard that it is a love letter in which Abingdon chides her for flirting with other men."

"Did Lawrence Abingdon want to marry her?"

"It is hard to know whether they were just playing at love. They certainly did not have a normal courtship. No respectable woman would be in a situation like hers and no respectable man would want to marry a woman who lived as she did. But women like her do get married. Sometimes they achieve a kind of respectability. Life is very strange, especially here in New York."

The very next day Charlotte discovered something even more surprising about Susan's life. Rowena came to the boarding house after school and she had a request for Charlotte.

"Do you think you could find it in your heart to meet Susan's sister and her child?" she asked.

"Why does Susan's sister want to meet me? I don't know her. I did not even know Susan. You must know her though. Why does she want to meet me?"

For the first time Charlotte saw Rowena looking embarrassed, but only for a moment. She tossed her head and said pertly, "Susan's sister has come to the city from Schenectady with a young child. She is a very respectable

woman and wants a quiet place to stay while she sees that
Susan has a decent burial."

"Why did she bring her child?" Charlotte wondered.
"Wouldn't it have been better to leave her child with her
husband?"

"It's not her child. It is Susan's son. The sister—her
name is Anne Carter—has been taking care of him ever
since he was born, but she and her husband are not
wealthy and they want to discover whether Susan left
any money or provision for her child. Will you put in a
good word for her with Mrs. Richardson so she'll be able
to stay here for a few days?"

Later, when Charlotte told Daniel about Anne Carter
coming to stay at the boarding house, he was concerned
for Charlotte's safety.

"What if whoever killed Susan has a grudge against
her whole family? Will Mrs. Carter be safe in New York?
Even more important to me—will you be safe? I cannot
stand by and see you put yourself in danger by sheltering
a stranger."

Charlotte was touched by Daniel's concern for her,
but she dismissed his worry. "Susan's life in New York
was quite separate from the life of her sister. I hardly
think there can be any danger in helping a bereaved
sister. Why don't you stay and meet Mrs. Carter?
Perhaps that will help us judge whether Susan's death has
any connection to her family."

When Anne Carter appeared she was dusty and
disheveled from her long ride on the railroad and the

Hudson River boat. Her gray homespun dress looked worn and her plain black bonnet drooped. The small blond boy who clutched her skirt looked as tired as she did. When Charlotte invited them to sit down, the boy clung to the woman's skirt and hid his face.

"I have made this long trip to the city, Miss Edgerton, to find out what happened to my sister. My husband told me I shouldn't come. That Susan had fallen on evil ways and we should pay her no heed, but she was my sister and I owe her something." Despite her fatigue, Anne Carter was clearly a woman of determination.

"I always had to take care of her when she was small," Mrs. Carter continued "and she was a handful. She could have married young Jacob Smith who was the foreman on a farm over toward Albany, but she would have none of it. She wanted to be free she said. As if any decent woman is ever free."

Mrs. Carter paused and put a handkerchief to her eyes. "When the traveling theatrical group came through town she managed to sneak off and see the show. Then she said some actor fellow promised she could get an acting job if she came to New York. After that there was no holding her. She was going to get to the city come what may. And get here she did.

"As for that acting fellow, he soon disappeared. And it seemed like acting jobs weren't as easy to get as Susan thought. She talked big in her letters, but finally she had to take a job as a housemaid in one of those mansions. She was a sweet talker was Susan, and she talked some rich woman into giving her a job even though she had no references. But I'm afraid she was too sweet-talking for her own good.

"She wrote to me and said one of the men she had met at the house thought she was the prettiest girl around; 'blooming' he called her and a 'sweet country maid'. Susan seemed to think he would love her forever and take care of her, but I could of told her that would never happen. Next thing you know she was in trouble and came running back to me. Came up to Schenectady and expected my husband and me to take care of her and the baby. Well we did. What else could we do? My Henry is a good man and we have no children of our own. Susan barely stayed with us long enough to wean the baby and then she slipped back to the city again. And you can see where that led her. At least we have Johnny and a sweet-tempered child he is. No, we'll never regret taking Johnny, but I want to do right by my sister too."

Charlotte and Daniel were overwhelmed by this information, but they knew it was important to find out what connection it might have to Susan's death. "Did Susan continue to be in contact with the man, and with the family she worked for?" Daniel asked.

"No, I don't believe she did. She was ordered to leave the house in no uncertain terms as I understand it. Susan never told anyone the name of the man responsible. She never told me his name either. But I knew it must be the young man who said she was so pretty and blooming. My husband and I certainly never encouraged her to talk about what happened. We didn't want to hear about such sinfulness. My father-in-law is a preacher and he would have objected to us having Susan in the house if he thought there was any of that kind of talk."

"Did you hear from Susan often after she came back here to the city?" Charlotte wanted to know.

"She sent gifts sometimes—toys and jackets for the child. Last Christmas she sent a lovely spinning top. We tell Johnny the gifts are from Aunt Susan. But she doesn't often write letters. Not that I would want to have letters about such goings-on. Leave city living to the city, I say."

"When was Johnny born?" Daniel asked.

"It is almost three years ago now. He was born on December 2, 1840. Susan left our house shortly after the new year started. I never saw her after that—just a handful of letters to remember her by."

Anne Carter's face was drawn and pale. Johnny, who was now on her lap, had fallen fast asleep. It had been a long day for both of them and the woman was too exhausted to answer more questions. Besides, it was getting close to the time when Mrs. Richardson wanted all male guests out of the house. Daniel left and the women made their way upstairs.

CHAPTER NINE

A Noise in the Night

*That laughing eye, whose sunny beam
My memory would not cherish less; --
And oh, that smile! whose joyous gleam
Nor mortal language can express.*

Friday, November 24, 1843

Daniel walked quickly up the quiet streets toward his boarding house. The weather had turned cold and there was a hint of snow in the air. On Broadway the shops were lit with gas lamps and taverns were noisy with the voices of men arguing and joking. The sound of piano music from one house floated on the air. As Daniel passed by he saw a man walk up the steps and lift his cane to knock on the door, but just as he did that, the door burst open and a woman ran out screaming.

The man who had been about to knock on the door faded quickly away as Daniel watched, but the woman was still in front of the house. She had grown quiet and was sobbing into a handkerchief. Daniel walked over to her.

"Are you all right? Did someone hurt you? Is there a fight?"

"No, no. It's not me. It's Polly, poor Polly—she's just lying there. I'm sure she is dead. Mrs. Walker was standing by her door looking in and I peeked over her shoulder. Polly was lying on the floor, as still as could be. I didn't see any blood or anything, but she's not breathing." The woman began sobbing and turned to go back into the house.

By this time several other women were clustered around the door. Two night watchmen were puffing as they arrived from their watch post down on the next block. An older woman started telling them what had happened and the watchmen soon herded all of the women back into the house. Daniel saw a few men leaving the house quietly, looking rather embarrassed at the commotion and clearly not in the mood for questions, but no one paid any attention to them. Daniel guessed that the older woman was the owner of the house, so he introduced himself to her. "My name is Daniel Gallagher and I am a reporter. I'd like to ask you about what has happened here tonight."

"I am Louisa Walker," she answered, "I can't talk to you now. The watchmen are here."

Daniel started toward the door with the watchmen. "You can't come in here," warned one of them.

"I am a reporter," Daniel insisted, but no argument would get him into the house. He would have to wait until the next day and see whether some of the women would talk.

The next morning Daniel knocked on the door as early as he dared. It was opened by an elderly, cross-looking maid who looked as though she would like to turn him away, but Mrs. Walker appeared in the hall behind her and beckoned him in. She was dressed in a quiet morning dress of light blue linen, and her hair, which had been carefully coifed the night before, streamed carelessly over her shoulders. On her feet were soft slippers and in her hand a cup of tea. She was not dressed for visitors, but she nodded and led Daniel into the parlor.

"Are you determined to make a newspaper story of poor Polly's death?" she asked.

"The people of the city deserve to know what is going on. How else can they protect themselves against crime and violence? Please tell me what you know about this woman's death. You say her name was Polly?" He pulled out his notebook and prepared to take down the information.

"Yes, Polly Gladstone she was. I knew her for years; she was a fine woman, kind to everyone and always cheerful. Her voice was lovely and she often entertained us with her singing. She was a good girl..." the woman put a handkerchief to her eyes and sobbed a bit but soon gathered herself together and continued. "She came from someplace on Long Island. Huntington, I believe. She kept in touch with her family there. Polly frequently visited them and that is where she boarded her son."

"How long did she live in this house? Do you know how old her son is?"

"She has had a room with me since the boy was a few months old. Before that I knew her because she had elegant rooms on Chatham Street. She had a protector who kept her in great style. She visited the same dressmaker that I did and we became quite friendly. After her son was born she asked me whether she might move here. I do not know what happened to her gentleman friend." Mrs. Walker replied demurely. "Her son must be four or five years old. Oh, what will become of him now?"

"Do you have any idea who might have committed this terrible crime? Had anyone quarreled with Miss Gladstone? Was anything stolen from her room? Perhaps it was a robbery and she fought against the intruder." Daniel pulled out his notebook.

"Polly had a visitor last night. He is a man who has been here many times before and is a particular friend of Polly's. Of course, I am not at liberty to give you the names of any of our visitors, Mr. Gallagher. Many of the most important men in the city come to visit my girls and we would never betray their confidence."

"Do you remember what time this man arrived?"

"I am not sure, but it seems to me I heard the clock strike 8:00 soon after he came in. He said a few words to me in the parlor and then went upstairs with Polly. I thought I heard him leave later in the evening, but I could not be sure of that. Other people were coming and going and I did not pay particular attention.

"At about eleven o'clock I went upstairs and noticed Polly's door was ajar. I knocked and heard no answer, so I gently pushed the door open. There was poor Polly on the floor." Once again Mrs. Walker took out her handkerchief. "Oh, I never shall forget the sight of her lying there so still. She looked beautiful."

Daniel knew he had to write a story about this new atrocity in the city. Mrs. Walker was not going to allow him upstairs to view the scene of the crime, but at least he had some information about the victim and that was a start. He decided to go to the Hall of Justice and see whether the watchmen had found any evidence of who the culprit might be.

When Daniel entered the Tombs and asked whether he could talk to anyone who was in charge of solving this mystery, he was greeted by one of the watchmen he had seen the night before.

"Are you back again?" the man asked Daniel with a scowl. "Why are you so interested in Miss Polly? I'm beginning to think you have a suspicious interest in these cases. Weren't you also at the house where Susan Jones was killed? How did you happen to be on the spot for both of those?"

"I am a newspaperman, sir. My interest in these cases is that of anyone who lives in New York. Women in our city will not feel safe while there are murderers prowling about on the loose. It was purely a coincidence that I was close-by when the alarm was sounded for Polly Gladstone's death."

The watchman, a large, swaggering man who looked as though he might have served in the militia when he was younger, glared suspiciously at Daniel. His companion from the night before who walked over to join the conversation was a little friendlier.

"Will you be putting our names in the paper, young man?" he asked with a grin. "Make sure you get them right. My wife will be pleased to see that I've been keeping the city safe and getting some notice for it. Most people think we waste our time keeping the watch, but it is important."

After that the conversation was easier. Daniel learned that the doctor, the same one who had examined Susan Jones, said Polly had been strangled just as Susan had. But whoever had done it did not attempt to set fire to the body. As to why Polly hadn't screamed or made some noise, the watchmen thought she must have known her attacker and have been unafraid of him.

"Do you think the same man might have committed both crimes? Was there any connection between the two women?" Daniel wanted to know.

"No connection that we know of except that they were both sporting girls. Both of them were often seen on Broadway and around town. Women like that are always at risk because they don't marry and stay home like women should. They deserve what they get—that's my opinion. They're sinners all of them." The scowling watchman sounded as though he had no pity in him.

"What difference does it make if it was the same man?" asked the other watchman.

"You've already arrested a man for killing Susan Jones, but if the two murders were committed by the same man then Lawrence Abingdon cannot be to blame. There is sure to be a call for his release, isn't there?" Daniel could predict a loud protest if people thought an innocent man was being held in prison. And Lawrence Abingdon was not unknown—he had friends and many people knew him through his writing.

"The police will determine who needs to be arrested and who doesn't, young man. And if you keep poking your nose into city business, you may find yourself in a cell too."

Daniel decided to go back to the house where Polly had been killed to see what else he could learn from Mrs. Walker or the other women who lived there. On his way there he stopped into a tobacco shop to buy a guidebook to city brothels. Perhaps he could talk to some of the women who lived in them and find out whether they had suffered any violence recently. He had no difficulty buying a copy of *Prostitution Exposed* and the shopkeeper chuckled wickedly as he handed it over, saying "Enjoy yourself young man, but keep a close watch on your purse."

Daniel slid the small book inside his jacket. He would read it later in the privacy of his own room, but first he would return to the house where Polly Gladstone died and try to interview some of the women who might be able to tell him more about the crime. Mrs. Walker, now dressed for afternoon callers, didn't hesitate to let him in. Five women were in the parlor; one was playing the piano, another was busy with needlework and the rest were lounging in chairs waiting for visitors. All of them were willing to talk to Daniel.

"Polly had not an enemy in the world," one of them said. "Put that in your newspaper! There are strangers coming into the city and preying upon us women. We have a right to earn a living the same as everyone else."

"How's a poor girl to get along if she doesn't have gentlemen friends?" asked another. "Mrs. Walker keeps an honest house and there's no one should try to drive us out."

"The best hope you have for finding out who is committing these crimes is to tell me about them so the public will know what's going on," Daniel pointed out. "I want to ask a few questions so that we can tell people. How long have you known Polly Gladstone?"

"Oh, quite a long time. She had been here for three or four years I think. She was here when I moved in. She has been saving money to open a brothel of her own. That's what she told me."

"Yes," agreed another woman. "She wanted to earn a lot of money. She had a son and she told me she was going to do her best for him. She wanted him to become an educated gentleman. That's what she said. I don't know what will happen to the poor boy now."

Daniel could sympathize with Polly's ambitions for her son. She had the instincts of any parent. Who would have wanted to hurt her? Mrs. Walker had said nothing was stolen, but was she right about that?

"Polly must have had some money if she was saving up to start a brothel. Do you know where she kept her money?" The women looked at him blankly and no one answered.

"Maybe one of her gentlemen friends kept her money for her," one woman suggested. "Polly wasn't one to buy very much jewelry. She liked to have cash, but I'm not sure she would have kept it in her room."

"Did any of her other gentlemen friends visit her last night? Were there many people here?" Daniel asked.

The woman who had been playing the piano was still trailing her fingers across the keys, but she had stopped playing. "It was a very quiet day yesterday. At least we got the piano tuned. I spent part of the afternoon here in the parlor watching the tuner working on the piano. I love music."

"I can see that you do," Daniel replied politely. "Do you know the name of the man who tuned your piano?"

"Oh, that is James Jackson. He comes quite often to work on this piano. Mrs. Walker thinks highly of him and so do many of the other brothel keepers."

James Jackson, Daniel thought. He had been on the scene when Susan Jones was killed too. Was it possible there was a connection? It was not a thought Daniel welcomed. He had liked the man when he met him at the rally and he knew Charlotte was friendly with Mrs. Jackson. But why was he so often close by when something terrible happened?

CHAPTER TEN

No End to Troubles

We have made a covenant with death, and with hell are we at agreement.

Monday, November 27, 1843

Charlotte woke on Monday morning to the sound of rain pelting on her small window. She could feel the chill wind coming through the window frame as she huddled in her bed. Ever since Daniel had told her about Polly Gladstone's death she had been wondering whether she had made a mistake coming to New York. Last year she had lived through the disruption and sorrow caused by one violent death in her close-knit community, but this bustling city was filled with frightening crimes and threatening strangers. When she went downstairs for breakfast she read the story Daniel had written for the newspaper:

It is no wonder that the city is excited about the announcement by the police today that another young woman has been wantonly murdered in our city. Miss Polly Gladstone was found strangled last night in her own room. The murder of Susan Jones, just a few days ago shocked all New Yorkers and news of the event traveled as far as Brooklyn and Connecticut. More excitement ensued when a young man from a respectable family was arrested for the crime. Was it possible that such a young man, already becoming famous for his writings, which have appeared in major journals, could be responsible for such a sordid crime?

And now what do we hear? While this same young man is being held in the gloomy dungeon that we call the Tombs, another young woman, not unlike Susan Jones, has been strangled in another part of the city. How could this happen? Surely our prisoner could not have leapt from his cell to commit such an atrocity. And yet the crimes are so similar that they appear to be the work of one man. Even in a large city like New York we cannot believe there two such depraved creatures.

Is it possible that the police made a mistake in arresting Lawrence Abingdon? Was that young man guilty of nothing more than being in the wrong location on the fatal night? Perhaps he is innocent of any crime. In that case the city owes him and his family an apology.

But more important than that is a greater task. The police of our great city must work untiringly to catch the perpetrator of these crimes and put him behind bars. All of the citizens of our city cry out to them to save other women—and perhaps men too—from this villain.

It was a stirring story and Charlotte was proud of Daniel for having written it. But she shivered when she thought of someone stalking the women of the city. Perhaps next time he would strike her or another innocent woman walking down a street just as she walked back and forth to her school. She knew the police would have a very hard time trying to identify the criminal. Where would they start?

Under pressure from his influential friends, the police released Lawrence Abingdon from prison, warning him not to leave the city. He made no statement when he was released, but disappeared into his solitary room. Would he ever reappear to read his poetry in Mrs. Brown's parlor?

The weather had turned colder and a sleety rain was drenching the streets, turning them into muddy tracks by the time Charlotte left the boarding house. She gathered her cloak around her shoulders and clutched the hood to keep her hair dry. As she plodded through the squishy mud trying to avoid splashes as horses drove past, she hoped the bad weather wouldn't keep too many of the children at home. Many of them had neither warm winter clothing nor sturdy shoes. If the trustees were raising money to provide warmer clothing, they had better hurry and do it.

When she reached the school, Charlotte found Mercy Jackson looking worried as she prepared to receive the children. Monday morning when the children came back from a break in their week of school they were always more restless than usual. Charlotte hoped the children would remember the song she had taught them the week before.

> Twinkle, twinkle little star
> How I wonder what you are.
> Up above the world so high,
> Like a diamond in the sky.

The children loved singing of any kind and after finishing the familiar song they had enjoyed thinking of other things that stars looked like—candles, gaslights, sparks. Charlotte hoped they would remember the verse and enjoy talking about it a little more. Their chatter might even cheer her up and relieve the heavy fear that gripped her. She wrote the words carefully on her slate so they would see it when they came into the room.

Later, as Charlotte watched the children file into her classroom, she was surprised to see that James Jackson was also at the school helping his wife move the children's long benches in her classroom. He often brought his mouth organ when he came to the school and Charlotte hoped he would play a few songs for the students. It would be a nice surprise on a gloomy Monday morning.

About an hour later, Charlotte heard men's voices in the hall. At first she couldn't understand the words but then she heard James Jackson's voice, "I protest this great injustice..." The children huddled together on their benches, afraid of the noise outside. Heavy boots tramped through the hallway and the front door closed with a bang.

The disturbance was too much for Charlotte. She opened the door and peered into the hall. John Fox was standing outside his office door looking distressed, while Mercy Jackson towered over him, her dark face creased with anger and pain.

Charlotte took a step toward them, wondering whether she should interrupt, but when Mercy Jackson turned her anguished face toward her, she spoke out. "What has happened? Where is your husband?"

Mercy remained silent, but Mr. Fox spoke quietly. "Mr. Jackson has been arrested for the murder of a woman called Polly Gladstone. They say he was in the house where she was killed and though he pretended to tune the piano, he was secretly plotting a crime."

"That's impossible!" cried Charlotte. "He wouldn't do anything like that."

"No indeed he would not," stated Mercy Jackson in a cold, loud voice. "Is New York just as bad as Virginia where colored men can be dragged off to prison for no crime at all? Is this what freedom means? The Lord will not abide it."

For a few minutes everyone was silent. Charlotte dimly noticed the faces of the students hovering in the doorways of classrooms. Then finally it was Mercy who spoke. "I am going to pray with my students for the relief of this injustice. Later I will go down to the Tombs and see what they are doing to my husband."

"I will do the same," Charlotte decided quickly. "We should go together to be sure your husband is being treated well and to correct the great injustice that is being done."

The rest of the school day was spent in Bible stories and prayers. When it was finally time to send the children home, Charlotte and Mercy wrapped themselves in their warm cloaks and set off for the Tombs. By then the mud had frozen into dirty ice. As they left Broadway and turned into the Bowery, the scene grew shabbier. Charlotte looked into shops that sold cheap readymade clothes for women who had no time to sew their own and no money to pay a seamstress. Many of the doorways led to taverns decorated with signs saying "Oysters in Every Style." The tables were filled with workmen getting a bite to eat after their day's work.

Finally they came to a large stone building with elegant Egyptian-style columns at the top of a flight of granite steps. As they entered the building they found themselves in a long hallway leading to a large open gallery. Looking up they could see four levels of cells facing the gallery. Each tier was patrolled by a uniformed guard.

At the large desk on the main floor a clerk grudgingly told them that James Jackson was in a cell on the lowest level. "We keep all the colored men down on that level," the man remarked. "They don't complain about the stench from the old cow pond underneath the building."

A guard led Charlotte and Mercy to the cell and opened the door for them. "You can have ten minutes to see your man," he told Mercy. "Then I'll come back and you will have to leave."

James Jackson was sitting on the edge of a narrow cot, his head in his hands. The cell was dim—the only light came through a small chink high on the wall. On one side of the cot was a small wash stand holding a dirty bowl with no water in it. When the women came in Jackson stood up to welcome them. He didn't look at all like the cheerful man Charlotte had seen at the political rally. His face was as stern as Mercy's and his words echoed hers.

"Have we returned to Virginia? Has New York no justice left? I did not expect such harsh treatment at the hands of officials in this city. I have to call upon the Lord and cry out in the voice of the prophets, Vindicate me, O God, and defend my cause against an ungodly people, from the deceitful and unjust man deliver me!"

"Even the Lord probably cannot see into this dismal place," said Mercy briskly. "We can cry out to the Lord as much as we want, but the sheriff will not believe you are innocent until the real criminal is caught."

"What makes the sheriff think that you are guilty?" asked Charlotte.

"Only the fact that my work takes me into most of the brothels of the city. How can I not go to those? They are often the only people who have the money to buy pianos and piano tuning is my trade. I must earn a living to provide for my wife and son.

"The watchmen thought it was suspicious that I was tuning the piano so late in the evening, but when I went there earlier in the day, someone was playing the instrument. Mrs. Walker asked me to return later. I came back when the parlor was quiet and worked on the piano until the sound was right. Then I left and went home."

"Did you see anyone else at the house?" Charlotte wanted to know.

"A few men came in and spoke briefly to Mrs. Walker. They must have gone upstairs because no one came into the parlor."

"And who saw you out when you left?" Charlotte pursued the questioning. "Whoever that was can testify you were not in the house when the crime occurred. We need to speak…"

As she was talking, one of the guards came to the cell. He unlocked the door and pulled it open. "Time's up, ladies. You must leave now."

Charlotte started to beg for more time, but the guard only frowned fiercely and gestured her toward the door. Mercy grasped her husband's hands silently, murmured something to him, and followed Charlotte out without looking at the guard. She held her head high and paid no attention to the other prisoners who stared at the women from their cells.

It was a relief to get out of the squalid prison and into the fresh, chilly air of the street, but they knew no more about the crime than when they had entered the Tombs. Where could they turn now?

CHAPTER ELEVEN

The Last of Susan

Golden lads and girls all must,
As chimney-sweepers, come to dust

Tuesday, November 28, 1843

Tuesday afternoon Charlotte hurried back to the boarding house to find Mrs. Carter and learn more about Susan. Anne Carter had been unwilling to talk with Daniel or even to see him. She was suspicious of all journalists and very much afraid her husband would be angry about any scandal. Soon she would be leaving New York and taking Johnny with her. This was Charlotte's only chance to find out more about whether Susan had any enemies. Mrs. Carter was very willing to help solve the mystery. Susan's death had frightened her. She feared for both herself and young Johnny.

"Have you been able to get Susan's belongings and settle her affairs?" Charlotte asked.

"Oh yes, Mrs. Brown was very helpful. Susan had a lot of lovely jewelry. She had a diamond bracelet. Can you imagine that? I had never seen such a bracelet. And a fancy gold ring and several pairs of earrings. Mrs. Brown helped me to sell those as well as some of Susan's dresses. Miss Scott bought some of her jewelry and we found a shop on the Battery where the man was happy to buy such lovely pieces. At least now I have some money to take care of poor Johnny and a few mementoes of his mother. He will cherish those when he grows older."

"Did you find any letters, or books, or perhaps pictures that gave you any idea of the people Susan knew or why anyone would try to harm her?"

"That's what the watchmen asked me. One of them looked at all of Susan's belongings, but I don't believe he found anything of interest—only a book of poetry by that man Lawrence Abingdon. But now I hear that he has been released. The police don't believe he had anything to do with Susan's death. I gave the poetry book to Miss Scott. We don't go in for that kind of poetry in Schenectady."

"Were there any letters from Mr. Abingdon? Or from anyone else?"

"There were a few letters from Mr. Abingdon, but they were not ones I would want to save for Johnny. The watchmen took those away. Not that they are of any use. I don't think Johnny will want to know how his mother lived. I had hoped there might be something to let us know who Johnny's father is, but there was nothing.

"When Susan came home after she got into trouble—our mother was still alive then—Susan put a brave face on it. She said she would take care of her son herself and never let a man bully her into doing something she didn't want to do. 'You can't trust in any man's promises' she declared. 'I know what's right for Johnny and I'll see that he gets a proper upbringing. When I get together some money I'll see he has a fine education. He'll be a great man someday.' Now look what has happened! But poor Susan wasn't a bad girl. She was trying to do the best she could."

Anne Carter stopped talking to wipe away the tears that were sliding down her cheeks. "That's all I have to tell you. Tomorrow I am going to make sure Susan is decently buried and then we will go back home. The only time I ever want to come back to this city is to see that a proper stone is placed on Susan's grave. Johnny is my son now and perhaps the less said about his mother the better. May she rest in peace!"

When Charlotte told Daniel about her conversation with Mrs. Carter, he decided to attend the burial. Mrs. Carter wanted Susan to be buried in an Episcopalian cemetery, but the familiar one at Trinity Church was now overcrowded; no more burials could take place there. Rowena Scott had generously purchased a plot for Susan in the new burying ground at St. John's Church. She had even hired a carriage to drive Anne Carter, Johnny, and her the mile or so up there. When Daniel told them he would like to attend, they offered to share the carriage.

As they drove north toward the edge of the city, the carriage bumped over dirt roads and there were few houses. The fields lining the road were brown and quiet; they saw only an occasional farmer in the distance working around his barn. The new church, when they finally reached it, stood alone in a bare brown churchyard. A few shrubs had been planted near the church entrance, but they were skinny and leafless on this cold November day. The burial ground was bleak. Withered leaves had fallen from the trees that dotted the plots and a sparse sprinkling of gravestones were the only reminders that other people had already been buried at this lonely spot.

There was no proper funeral. The church was willing to sell a grave site, but did not offer to conduct a service for someone so notorious. No minister presided, no prayers were said, and no one spoke about the dead woman. Two gnarled old grave diggers lowered the cheap pine coffin into the grave and shoveled dirt over it. They removed their caps for a moment in a brief tribute to the dead woman and then left without looking back.

When the gravediggers left, Daniel and the two women stood next to the barren grave site. Daniel worried that Mrs. Carter would feel cheated by the lack of a ceremony. "I'll say a prayer for your sister," he said abruptly and started murmuring "Our Father Who art in heaven..." Rowena and Mrs. Carter joined in and little

Johnny stood between the two women and bowed his head.

"We should sing a hymn," Rowena suggested and began to sing in a sweet, thin voice:

The Lord's my shepherd, I'll not want;
He makes me down to lie
In pastures green; he leadeth me
The quiet waters by.

My soul he doth restore again,
And me to walk doth make
Within the paths of righteousness,
E'en for his own name's sake.

Yea, though I walk in death's dark vale,
Yet will I fear no ill:
For thou art with me, and thy rod
And staff me comfort still.

When Rowena stopped singing, Mrs. Carter turned briskly away, satisfied that her duty to Susan was finished. Daniel had hoped someone else would be at the funeral. Some friend perhaps who might know more about Susan than he had been able to learn. But the cemetery was empty. A chill wind blew through the trees as the small group walked back to the carriage.

Daniel wondered how Anne Carter felt. Her stiff demeanor puzzled him. He knew how he would feel if one of his sisters had been buried so unceremoniously. He stepped forward. "I am sorry for your loss, Mrs.

Carter. I would like to write a short tribute to your sister for my newspaper. May I call on you this evening? Perhaps you can give me more details about her."

"Oh, I cannot talk to you about Susan. My husband made me promise I would not speak to any reporter for fear it might cause scandal and injure the family. I was afraid he would forbid me to come down here. Your friend Miss Edgerton asked me many questions last night. You had better talk to her."

Rowena spoke up brightly. "Perhaps you should pay me a visit. I have known Susan for these past two years and she confided in me many times. But this is not the time or place. I will go to Miss Edgerton's boarding house later and there we can talk."

Before the time came to meet Rowena, Daniel wanted to write a story about James Jackson and how he had been arrested. The newspapers had carried only a brief mention of that. Both reporters and editors knew the public was far less interested in the detention of a former slave than they were in the arrest of a prosperous poet from a good family. James Jackson had been right in saying that New York was like Virginia. No one believed the life of a colored man was as important as that of a white man.

When he returned to the newspaper office, Daniel wrote a story about James Jackson's life and his sudden arrest. He looked it over with satisfaction when he had finished and hoped the editor would not cut it drastically before printing the paper:

This great city was shocked again yesterday by the death of a well-known woman of the city. She was strangled in her bed in a well-known house on Mercer Street. Just like Susan Jones only a week ago, Polly Gladstone died quickly and violently. Authorities believe that the same villain probably murdered both of these women. There has been a man arrested in the case, a man named James Jackson who is a piano tuner and who has worked in many of the city's taverns and sporting houses. He had previously been a slave in the state of Virginia, but his master made provision in his will to free all of his slaves. Jackson and his wife then moved to New York City where they have lived for almost twenty years. The man has not been in trouble before, but authorities believe that his work might have led to his familiarity with vice and into temptation and sin. No date has been set for his trial.

Daniel sighed as he handed his article to the editor. If it was printed as he had written it, surely many people would see there was almost no evidence to connect Jackson to the crimes. Would anyone protest the arrest? Would there be a public outcry if the case ever came to court?

That evening both Charlotte and Daniel were glad to have a chance to talk to Rowena again. She was the person who knew most about Susan's life in New York. There must have been some clues about Susan's friends and who might have quarreled with her. When Rowena came over the three of them clustered together in the parlor.

"Did Susan ever talk to you about her son?" Charlotte asked.

"She didn't say much, although she sometimes showed me toys she had bought to send to the child. She said that Johnny was being well taken care of and that when she had enough money saved, she would bring him to New York. She was very proud to think she could take care of him."

"Did she ever talk about the father of the child?" Charlotte probed cautiously.

"Once she did. She got a letter once that made her very angry. I saw her crying about it in her room. She said 'that odious man'—that is what she called him—had told her he was going to bring the sheriff to take the child away from her. He said Susan was immoral and had no right to keep the child."

"She must have been frightened by that." Daniel suggested.

"Oh Susan was not easily frightened. She said she could outwit him. Neither he nor anyone else knew where the baby was. She trusted her sister to keep the child safe. Mrs. Carter and her husband are very respectable people and no one could object to a child being raised by them."

"But who was the man? Did she say? Did she say anything about him?" Charlotte persisted.

"He was someone in the family that she worked for when she first came to the city. That rich family who lived in Washington Square. She said the woman who hired her was nice at first. She was fussy about turning the sheets exactly right and always saw every speck of dust left in a room, but Susan didn't complain much about her.

"Susan was pretty girl and the house was full of young men. There were sons and cousins and sons-in-law and they often pestered the maids. 'Never trust a rich young man' Susan said to me. She said the reason she liked being a sporting girl was that men had to pay instead of making promises. 'I'd never go back to being a servant again' she said."

"But it was the mother who made Susan leave, wasn't it?"

"Yes, it's always the woman who has to keep order. Mrs. Whoever-it-was wouldn't hear a word against her sons. She acted as though Susan had gotten herself with child. And she sent Susan packing with nothing but her last quarter's pay. Susan was lucky she had a sister to go to. If it had been me I would have gone to Madam Denis and gotten rid of the baby, but Susan wouldn't hear of that."

After Rowena left, Charlotte turned to Daniel. "Neither Rowena Scott nor Mrs. Carter know the family Susan worked for, but it must have been the Van Pelts. She must be the same Susan your sister told me about when I first met her. The one who came back to visit the staff at the house. Why don't we ask your sister to try to find out more about the Van Pelt family? If it was someone in the house who was involved with Susan, we need to know who it was."

"I don't want to ask Eileen to spy for us," Daniel objected.

"But she might be in danger," Charlotte countered urgently. "We must find out whether there is someone evil connected with the Van Pelt family."

CHAPTER TWELVE

Turmoil in the Tombs

Nobody knows the trouble I've seen
Nobody knows my sorrow

Wednesday, November 29, 1843

The week following James Jackson's arrest dragged on.
Charlotte watched Mercy Jackson trudging up the stairs
to the schoolhouse; she had lost her firm step and
cheerful aspect. Charlotte found it difficult to ask
questions. James Jackson was still being held in prison.
Hope for his timely release was growing dim. Justice
moved slowly and there was nothing friends or family
could do.

On Wednesday morning Mr. Fox asked Charlotte to
come into his office where he closed the door and said
quietly, "James Jackson has been a faithful worker in this
school as well as many other places across the city. It
grieves me to see him suffering in prison. Has Mrs.

Jackson said anything to you about what happened last week when that woman was killed?"

"She has said nothing except that her husband is not guilty. I believe her. He is an honest, hard-working man. Yesterday I talked with one of the women from the house where the first murder took place and she too found it difficult to suspect him."

"How do you know such a woman, Miss Edgerton?" Charlotte could see the shock in John Fox's face.

"The woman, Rowena Scott, came to stay at the boarding house where I live. She stayed for just a few days after the fire because her room was damaged. I assure you that my boarding house is most respectable and Miss Scott lived a very quiet and virtuous life while she was there. She is not a bad person, but only a young woman who has been led astray. And I believe we can trust what she says about Mr. Jackson."

Mr. Fox nodded gravely and Charlotte continued.

"Miss Scott has known James Jackson for several years. He tunes the pianos in many of the..." Charlotte hesitated over her choice of words, "many of the so-called sporting houses in the city. Sometimes he brings his son who dances and plays the mouth organ to entertain while his father plays the piano. She told me that Mr. Jackson has always been most respectful and is in turn respected by everyone who knows him. There is no reason to suspect he would be connected with a crime."

"That has always been my impression too," John Fox added. "I fear the police were very quick to seize on him. They are ignorant men who often assume that crimes in this city are committed by immigrants and colored people."

His voice became louder as he continued and he sounded more like a preacher, "Slavery is a terrible blot upon this country. It has corrupted many officials and citizens. I believe with William Lloyd Garrison that America has made a covenant with death by allowing slavery to continue. Slavery has been abolished in New York, but the ill effects of it creep up from the Southern states and from our own history. I wonder whether we shall ever be free of it."

Charlotte went to her classroom and looked at her young pupils as they bent over their slates. She tried to imagine how they felt about being black when most of the children they saw around them were white. Had they already known the scorn so many white people heaped on them? She decided to read William Blake's poem about the little black boy to the class:

> *My mother bore me in the southern wild,*
> *And I am black, but oh my soul is white!*
> *White as an angel is the English child,*
> *But I am black, as if bereaved of light.*

"My soul is white too," boasted Kevin Washington, one of the older boys in her group.

"How do you know? You can't see you soul," retorted the boy sitting next to him. He shoved Kevin and laughed, but Kevin wouldn't budge.

"No one knows what color our souls are," Charlotte told them. "But I think we are all the same inside. When God looks at us he doesn't see the color of our skin. He sees whether we have been good or not."

"But people look at the outside. That's why the boy next door to us fights with me and my brother all the time. Yesterday he had a knife and he said he was going to scrape all the black off my face. But my father was coming home and he chased that boy away."

How early they had learned the lesson of how people looked at them. Even many of the abolitionists who wanted all the slaves freed did not believe Africans were the same as white people. But Charlotte couldn't cure everything that was wrong in the world. All she could do was to teach the students as well as she could so they could make a decent life for themselves if people would let them.

After school was over, Charlotte told Mercy she would like to walk down to the Tombs with her to visit James Jackson again. Mercy had not been able to find out what charges were being brought against him or when he was likely to have a trial. She wanted to find a lawyer, but so far had been unable to locate anyone willing to help the Jacksons and accept the low fee they could pay.

Once again the two women approached the gloomy building called the Tombs. They walked up the grim granite steps and through the door between the Egyptian columns. Mercy had been given a pass to see her husband, so she was waved into the building and Charlotte went with her. They walked quickly to the same cell they had visited before and asked the guard to let them in.

"You had better be careful," the guard said. "There are some prisoners here who have heard about the crimes your husband has been accused of. Some of them were shouting and a swearing that no colored man who had touched the hair on the head of an innocent white woman should be allowed to live."

Charlotte shuddered to hear those words, but Mercy looked as though the guard had not said anything. She waited silently while he unlocked the creaking door and walked in. Charlotte followed her. James Jackson was seated on the cot as he had been before. He stood up as the women came in and greeted them, but his smile was more like a grimace.

"Has there been any word about when the police will charge me?" he asked. "This place is intolerable and I am afraid for my life sometimes when the prisoners start shouting and clamoring for my death. Some of the guards feel the same way, I fear. Someday one of them will thrust a knife into my heart if I am kept in this place too long. They grow angrier by the day."

And indeed there was shouting and swearing. The sound was growing louder and voices rang clearly through the atrium.

"Kill the black man! We must keep our women safe!"

"Why am I kept in a place with these dumb Africans? White men ought to have a place of their own and not have to share our jail with riff-raff."

"Go back to the jungle where you belong!"

Clang! Clang! Clang! Some of the men started beating on the bars of their cells with their spoons. More and more began to do it and the sound became deafening. Worried guards scurried from cell to cell trying to see who had spoons and to confiscate them, but there were too few guards to gather all the spoons.

James Jackson put his arm around Mercy and leaned against the far wall of his cell. "Get back here, out of the way," he called to Charlotte who was peering through the small opening at the front of the cell.

Then came a sudden hush and a tramp of feet. Charlotte saw a tall figure in a militia uniform move toward the bridge in the center of the prison that crossed the open atrium. By his side were two policemen carrying rifles.

The man spoke in the loud voice of a leader. "There will be no food tonight for any prisoner. All of you will be punished for this breach of decorum. While I am commander of this prison we will have no riots and no unseemly behavior. Is that understood?"

The clanging ceased and was replaced by muttering. Slowly the sound ebbed away. All the men were silent now. Charlotte couldn't see their faces, but she knew they were staring sullenly at the commander. She could breathe freely again, but she felt limp and drained from the overwhelming emotional outbreak. She had never seen such fury and hatred before and she trembled to think what it might lead to. Was it true that some of the guards felt the same way the prisoners did? Would James Jackson be safe here? When would he be brought to trial?

Before they left the building Mercy asked the official at the desk when she would be able to learn more about her husband's trial. The official had little interest in giving information.

"Well, there's not much known about that. Jackson is being held on suspicion of loitering near the scene of a crime."

"Do you mean he has not been charged with a murder?" asked Mercy hopefully.

"There's no record of a murder charge here. The policeman who brought him in claimed he was responsible for the deaths of two young women, but the coroner's jury only determined that the woman..." He stopped to fumble with the papers on his desk. "Polly Gladstone was strangled. That is the cause of death, but no evidence has been submitted about who is responsible. The policemen took it on themselves to arrest James Jackson for loitering, as I said."

"But there were many people going in and out of the house where Miss Gladstone was killed," Charlotte interrupted. "Were they all arrested for loitering?"

"That ain't likely. We couldn't hold every man who visited a brothel." The man was scornful. "But some people look more suspicious than others."

"We know why it is you people think my husband looked suspicious," Mercy's voice was loud and indignant. "You think every colored man must be up to no good. But we will prove you wrong."

The two women were seething with anger as they left the building.

When Charlotte went to bed that night she could not sleep. The voices from the Tombs kept echoing in her ears. There had been anger in those voices and also fear. She shuddered to think how long it might take for those feelings to disappear—years and years of struggle before people learned to live together.

She remembered her days at Brook Farm, which seemed years ago instead of just a few months. She had listened to people like Lydia Child as she talked about how difficult it would be to abolish slavery. And even that would not be the end. The test, according to Child, would be when all Americans would "treat the man of color in all circumstances as a man and brother." How long would it take even in New York, where slavery had been abolished almost fifteen years ago, for men and women to do that?

As Charlotte tossed and turned trying to sleep; she remembered so many things from her Brook Farm days. She and the other members of the community had high hopes of reforming the world, but Charlotte knew she would never be able to do that. If only she could talk with some of the people who had shared that dream. If only she could talk with Margaret Fuller. At last there was a ray of hope!

Margaret Fuller wrote articles for the *Tribune*, just as Daniel did. But she seldom went to the newspaper offices. Instead, she lived north of the city in quiet Turtle Bay with the Greeley family. Perhaps it would be possible for Charlotte to call on her and get some ideas about how she could help James Jackson as well as the students in her school. With that hopeful idea in mind, she was able to fall asleep.

The next morning Charlotte wrote a note to Miss Fuller asking whether she might call on her. She would get the address from Daniel next time she saw him. Finding out who had killed Susan and Polly would be the key to getting James Jackson freed from prison, but improving the situation for all free blacks would prevent that kind of injustice from happening again.

School was quiet that day and neither Charlotte nor Mercy wanted to talk about their visit to the Tombs. Mercy's powerful shoulders were bent with care as she went about her duties in the classroom. When she and Charlotte sat down in the lunch room to eat, she shared some of her worries.

"Two of the children have been withdrawn from classes," she told Charlotte. "I am sure it is because people are afraid of my husband and the scandal that has come to the school. When Mr. Fox came to the classroom this morning, I was afraid he was going to tell me I must leave. But he said nothing about that."

"Surely he doesn't think your husband is guilty, does he?"

"I don't think he believes that, but if people stop giving money to the school, it cannot continue. No matter what Mr. Fox believes, he must have money to run the school."

"Perhaps Mr. Greeley's newspaper could help us raise money for the school," Charlotte suggested. "Many liberal people read his paper. We might be able to tell them about what has happened and ask for contributions. If only we had a way to call attention to the school and the work we are doing here."

Despite her worries, Charlotte was determined to visit Eileen that afternoon. She plodded along the wintery street up to Washington Square Park hoping to talk with her. As she approached the back door and was admitted into the warm kitchen, her spirits rose.

Eileen took Charlotte up to the tiny attic room so they could talk quietly for a few minutes, but she warned that they must not let any of the Van Pelts see them.

"I have talked with Susan Jones's sister," Charlotte began, "and she was sure that the father of Susan's son has some connection with the Van Pelt family. She didn't know the name of the people Susan worked for, but you and I know that it was here."

"That's possible," Eileen agreed. "The Van Pelts have many guests and Susan might have been foolish enough to let one of them have his way with her."

"Do you think it might have been one of the family? One of the sons perhaps?"

"That might happen," Eileen said slowly. "Sure Mr. Jacob, the older son, is a rather large and forceful man. There would be no arguing with him, I'm afraid."

"And what about the younger son, Charles Van Pelt? Didn't you tell me he was a handsome young man?

"Handsome he is, there's no doubt about that," Eileen smiled as she answered. "But he has been very respectful and kind to me. He would never take advantage of anyone. I am sure of that."

Charlotte was less certain. "Just be sure you are careful yourself. Your brother is worried about you and cares a great deal about your safety."

"I know how to take care of myself," Eileen proclaimed. "I may have grown up in Ireland, but I am fast becoming an American girl and a New York girl at that. Tell Daniel he doesn't have to worry about me! I'm not his baby sister anymore."

Eileen promised to see whether she could find out anything about who the father of Susan's son might be. Charlotte had to leave, but she was troubled because Eileen seemed so young and yet she seemed so sure nothing could happen to her. Charlotte hoped that was true.

CHAPTER THIRTEEN

Music and Questions

If I could have the [minstrel] show back again in its pristine purity, I should have little use for opera.

Friday, December 1, 1843

By the time Daniel left the newspaper office on Friday it was dark. The pools of light from gaslights on the street barely reached the ground. A hint of snow was in the air and Daniel could feel a few flakes striking his face and settling on his cap as he walked toward Pine Street. He had spent most of the afternoon writing short articles about the sale of land north of Washington Square. The city was growing so fast that some people predicted it would eventually cover all of the narrow Manhattan Island.

If New York grew to be as large as London, the city would need to solve the problem of its rising crime rate. Daniel walked slowly, looking down at his feet to avoid slippery mud, and occasionally punching his fist into his hand. He was getting nowhere in his attempt to find Polly Gladstone's killer. A murderer was wandering the streets and laughing at the bewildered police. The thought of it made Daniel angry. He had interviewed the policeman who arrested James Jackson, but they had no real evidence to go on. When they found a colored man who had been on the scene, they arrested him and didn't look further. At least that was Daniel's belief. Despite the enthusiasm for abolition among many New Yorkers, people were not fond of having freed slaves living among them. Many hoped abolition would mean all the former slaves would return to Africa or go to some other distant land.

Visiting the brothel where Polly Gladstone had been killed might give him a start on finding who, aside from James Jackson, had the opportunity to attack Polly. It was almost a week since she had died and the house would no longer be in mourning. It was not a private house, but a public entertainment site. Mrs. Walker could not afford to close the place for a period of mourning. When Daniel approached he saw the flicker of gaslight inside the house and heard the sound of the piano being played. He was admitted by an elderly woman wearing a black dress. She motioned him into the parlor where Mrs. Walker was sitting in a comfortable chair smiling broadly as she listened to the music young Freedom Jackson was playing on the piano while he sang.

Buffalo gals, won't you come out tonight?
Come out tonight, Come out tonight?
Buffalo gals, won't you come out tonight,
And dance by the light of the moon.

Five young women were scattered around the room along with three men. Most of them hummed along with the song and clapped heartily when Freedom finished.

"Show us a dance, Freedom," someone called out when the song was over. The boy obliged by pulling a mouth organ out of his pocket, getting up and standing on a part of the floor not covered by carpet and dancing. Tap and click went his heels in a new kind of dance Daniel had never seen before. It reminded him of the Irish step dances he had seen at home, but Freedom's dance was faster and wilder. He held his mouth organ in one hand and his other arm flew out from his side and waved above his head in time with the music.

When the dance was over, Freedom sat down in a chair next to Daniel. The group in the parlor was breaking up as couples slipped away upstairs. Mrs. Walker went back to the kitchen to check on refreshments leaving Daniel and Freedom alone in the room.

"How is your father?" Daniel asked.

Freedom's cheerful face grew somber. "He doesn't complain, but he is in a bad way. He's kept cramped in that small cell with nothing to do except worry about how me and my mother are getting along without him. He keeps asking when his trial will be coming up—if he is ever charged with a crime—but the police tell him they are still investigating. They won't let him out of the prison while they do that because they say he might run away."

"There are laws about how long a man can be held without being charged," insisted Daniel.

Freedom's answer was a mirthless laugh. "Laws don't mean much when white folks deal with coloreds. Well, they don't mean much anytime, I guess. The laws say people can't be held unless they are charged, but no one tells the police they have to release anyone. The police run the prison."

Daniel pushed to get more information. "I didn't know you played the piano here, Freedom. Were you here that night Polly Gladstone was killed?"

"I was here early in the evening. That's the time I usually come. Mrs. Walker says I put the gentlemen in a good mood and they stay longer and buy more champagne and presents for the women. She gives me twenty-five cents for playing—sometimes four bits if people really like it. And that helps my mother keep the house going. That school she teaches at doesn't pay much and neither does piano tuning.

"My father thinks I should get more education and find a steady job, but that ain't easy. I'd like to go on the stage. Have you ever seen a minstrel show? People can make lots of money in those. That's what I want to do. That's why I keep playing and practicing my dancing. The brothels are the only places that have pianos and give me a chance to practice. Everyone here is gone now, so I'm going around to a house on the Bowery that I know. I'd like to make a little more money before the night ends."

Mrs. Walker had come back from the kitchen by this time. She looked at Daniel as he sat alone in the parlor. "Wouldn't you like to meet one of our young ladies? I think Annie is just sitting in her room reading. You and she could have a nice talk about books. You being a newspaper man must be a great reader."

"Oh, no," Mrs. Walker" Daniel stammered. He could feel his face getting warm as he flushed. "I came here because I have work to do. I'd like to ask you some more questions about Polly Gladstone. Sure, why don't you let me treat you to a nice glass of champagne and you can tell me all about Polly. Our readers feel great sympathy for her and they want to know more about her. They also want to be sure her killer will be caught."

"We all want that. I'll be glad to tell you as much as I know. The girls and I are afraid to sleep in our beds these nights. Who knows who might be breaking in? I love the city but if things continue like this, I may just go back to New Jersey.

"Polly was a fine young woman. I've known her almost since she was a child. Most of the girls here have come to New York from other cities, or other countries, but Polly is a New Yorker born and bred. Her family was a sad one. Her mother used to work in that big hotel on Broadway, but she got consumption and coughed so much the customers complained. The family moved into a tiny room in the Five Points neighborhood. The mother just got weaker and weaker and couldn't take care of her children very well. Her husband was a drinker. He could never keep a job and finally one night he just disappeared. Polly thinks he was shanghaied onto a ship, but I don't know about that. He could just as easily have fallen into the river when he was in drink. The mother died soon after that and then the two younger children got cholera and died. Polly was on her own. She had to eat. She was afraid to steal, so she didn't have much choice. She was on the street almost before she was old enough to know what it was about.

"But she was a lucky one. By the time she was sixteen or so she found a man to take care of her. He was married, but he was fond of Polly and he put her up in a room over on Broadway. She was settled pretty well, although she was alone a lot of the time. Sometimes she came over to talk with me and some of the girls. When she finally parted with that man she moved in here."

Mrs. Walker stopped talking and put a handkerchief to her eyes. Daniel could understand her feeling sad about the girl. So many children in the city grew up alone. There wasn't enough work for everyone and men and women scrambled by as best they could but many of them couldn't stay away from the drink and the crime that was everywhere. Polly had done well to move up to a house like this. It was clean and tidy, with plenty of fuel and plenty of food to keep the women comfortable. It was certainly a step up from living in Five Points.

"She had a hard life, I'm sure. But was there anyone who disliked her? Was there anyone she was afraid of? Did she ever talk about that?"

"Polly was a strong woman and she took no nonsense. Once there was a man came to see her here who wanted to tie her to the bed post. She was so angry she chased him all the way downstairs and out the door. But he was a poor timid fool and he would never have had the nerve to come back here. But enemies, no I don't think so.

"She had a son, you know. The police asked about that and about who the father was. None of us have any idea who that might be. Polly was always very independent and determined to earn enough money to set up her own house and get her son an education. She didn't talk about any of that lovey-dovey nonsense some girls are so fond of."

"Where does the son live? He's not with her here surely, is he?"

"No, he is staying with a relative of hers on Long Island—she says he is as safe and happy as can be. She doesn't—didn't—want him anywhere close to this neighborhood. He wasn't so far away that she couldn't get out there to see him pretty often."

Daniel was getting discouraged. There didn't seem any clue to connect any individual to Polly. "Can you tell me exactly what happened on the night Polly died?" he asked.

"I've gone over this with the police already. That was a busy evening. There was a lot of singing in the parlor and everyone was having a good time. A man who said he was John Smith came in and he went upstairs with Polly. His name was no more John Smith than mine is, but lots of men don't like to give their real name. Afraid their wives will find out. Anyway I saw this Mr. Smith or whoever he was leave quite early, about ten o'clock.

"Then there was a big man with a beard came in and was sitting over there in the corner talking to Polly while we were singing. He looked familiar somehow, but I don't know why. He wasn't one of our regulars. And I never did hear his name. I don't even know whether he went upstairs with Polly. And I know I didn't see him leave. But the parlor was empty before midnight and the visitors had either left or had arranged to stay all night.

"Then later, like I told the police, I thought something was wrong, so I opened Polly's door and found her lying there." Mrs. Walker stopped talking and began sobbing into her handkerchief.

Daniel felt uncomfortable. He knew he'd have to find out the name of the mysterious man who spent so much time talking to Polly. People would be likely to remember a man with a beard. Not many men grew beards these days. Did anyone know his name? And why did he seem familiar to Mrs. Walker? There were lots of questions but no answers. He sighed and decided he'd have to give up for tonight.

CHAPTER FOURTEEN

Chance Encounters

If you have knowledge, let others light their candles in it.

Saturday, December 2, 1843

On many afternoons when Charlotte was walking home from school she would see Rowena on Broadway visiting some of the fancy dress shops along the street. In her lovely fur cape she paid no attention to the cold November weather. Charlotte sometimes thought she spent time on the streets just to show off her cape. Charlotte often walked along with her for a while, although she felt like a small gray moth next to a beautiful butterfly. What a long way she had come since she arrived in New York less than a month ago. She wondered what her friends from Brook Farm would think of her parading down the street chatting with a sporting girl who lived for nothing but pleasure. But Rowena wasn't as carefree as she looked.

"Sometimes I hate to go back to the house because I'm afraid the man who attacked Susan and Polly will come looking for someone else." She shook her head and looked worried. "Perhaps James Jackson is the guilty man. I'm not sure any more. I'm becoming suspicious of every man who comes into the house. Several of my friends say Jackson must be guilty. Perhaps they are right."

"I don't believe James Jackson is guilty no matter how many people think he is. He is a good man," Charlotte insisted.

"But if he is not the guilty man, then the killer is still on the streets. I would rather believe the killer is safely in prison. But I don't know what to think and I am still afraid. Why don't the police bring him to trial? Why are they waiting? Perhaps there is someone else out there. No one can feel safe."

Charlotte shivered. She understood how Rowena felt. Everyone was uneasy. But the police did nothing and neither Charlotte nor Daniel knew how to discover the identity of Polly's mysterious visitor. Was he the same man who had talked to Susan? Rowena could tell her little about Susan's friends and visitors. As Mrs. Walker had told Daniel, men often used false names when visiting a brothel, and the names were usually so common there was no way to trace them.

"We have a dozen John Smiths who come regularly," reported Rowena scornfully. "We have thin John Smiths, fat John Smiths, young ones and old ones. No one knows what their real names are and they rarely tell the women anything about themselves unless they become regular visitors and friends like Lawrence Abingdon."

"Have you seen Lawrence Abingdon since he left the prison? Does he still visit?"

"He came over late one afternoon last week but he did nothing but sit gloomily in the parlor. I asked him to read some of his poetry to us as he so often used to do, but he hung back and said he was not ready. I am sure he is sad, but it doesn't help to mope and make everyone else unhappy too. We still have to entertain people and earn a living."

Daniel had to earn a living too, so he could not spend all of his time searching for whoever was responsible for Susan's and Polly's deaths. He had his own life to live and he wanted to move on with that.

On Saturday morning the early post brought Charlotte a note.

Dear Miss Edgerton,

Mr. Greeley has given me tickets to go to see the Saturday performance of the Hutchison Family Singers. I am to write a story about them for the newspaper. Would you like to come with me? I understand that their performance is very rewarding.

With best regards,
Daniel Gallagher

Charlotte had heard that the Hutchison singers were well-known throughout New York and had traveled and performed in many other states too. Even if she had never heard of them before, the crowds walking toward the theater when she and Daniel arrived would have alerted her to their popularity. The two of them joined the throng entering and were shown to a seat on the parquet level of the theater. Their seats were not as elegant as the boxes where society people sat, but far more comfortable than the upper tiers of cheap seats. Charlotte looked with interest at the well-dressed men and women in the seats near them.

Bright lights lit up the theater and the stage and there was almost no room left as the time for the performance drew close. Many people were munching hunks of bread, roasted potatoes, or sharing slices of meat or cheese. Everyone looked cheerful and ready to be entertained. A man shouted "Bring them out!" and another added, "We want the music".

Finally a robust man in a velvet-trimmed jacket came on stage and introduced the singers: "Ladies and gentlemen, I give you the best-known and most popular singers in the world today. They come from the granite state of New Hampshire and have entertained world leaders in Washington and in London. They are American singers singing American songs and we are indeed lucky to have them here with us tonight."

Three men and a woman walked out on the stage, took a bow and started singing:

Ho! the car, Emancipation,
Rides majestic thro' our nation
Bearing on its train, the story
Liberty! a nation's glory.

Roll it along! Roll it along!
Roll it along! thro' the nation
Freedom's car, Emancipation.

Almost before they had started singing, men throughout the theater began to stomp their feet in time to the music and some of them sang along with the group. Many people in the audience knew the words and sang verse after verse with them. When the song ended, cheers and clapping began and continued for several minutes.

Daniel quickly started taking notes as Charlotte looked around the audience to watch the spectacle. She was surprised to see a familiar figure not far from where she and Daniel were sitting. Lawrence Abingdon was enjoying the music as much as anyone else and clapping and cheering loudly. Every now and then he paused to talk to a tall, dapper man next to him who sat balancing a cane in his hands. The man, like many men in the audience, had not removed his black slouch hat and that together with his small, pointed beard caught Charlotte's eye. He must have noticed her looking at him because he smiled slightly and nodded his head to her.

The Hutchinson family was singing another song now, one about the Granite State of New Hampshire, their native state. The audience was even more familiar with this song and clapped so much that the group repeated the entire song for them. When the show was over the audience slowly left the theater, reluctant to give up the music and face the dark streets. Their faces were flushed with enthusiasm and many of them hummed the songs under their breath as they left.

Charlotte and Daniel joined the crowd squeezing out the door and almost ran into Lawrence Abingdon and his friend.

"Good evening, Mr. Abingdon," Daniel greeted him. "I have been looking forward to a chance to talk with you. Might I suggest that you and your friend join us for a bite to eat? There is an oyster shop right around the corner where we will find mighty tasty oysters and a cool drink—or a warm one if you prefer."

After a quick glance at his friend, Mr. Abingdon accepted the invitation and the four of them walked to the tavern. Inside the air was heavy with cigar smoke and the smell of oysters cooking. Sawdust on the floor caught the worst of the spilled beer and ale, but it was slippery underfoot. Still, the room was warm and cozy with a fire burning in the massive fireplace against one wall. Daniel led the way to a small table in the corner and they sat down.

"Mr. Gallagher, may I introduce my friend Walt Whitman, editor of the *Brooklyn Eagle* in our sister city across the river."

"Oh, indeed, I have read your articles in the newspaper, Mr. Whitman. And I would like to introduce my friend Miss Charlotte Edgerton who was kind enough to accompany me to the theater tonight to give me her opinion of the Hutchison Family Singers."

"And what did you think of our famous singing group, Miss Edgerton?" asked Walt Whitman." Are you familiar with their music?"

"No, indeed, I do not know their music at all. And I have never heard any group sing in the kind of harmony they use. Although there was a woman in the group, I could not pick her voice out from the others. All of the voices blended together so subtly that it was like one voice."

"Yes, indeed, Miss Edgerton," Whitman responded enthusiastically. "They have created a new style of singing—a completely American style. They are true children of the granite state and true democrats. Their singing is much preferable to the arid European styles we so often hear."

"Are you a musician yourself?" asked Charlotte.

Lawrence Abingdon interrupted with a laugh. "No, no, not a musician, but like myself a poet and writer. Mr. Whitman has written stories and poems, although many of them have not yet been published. When they are, he will be famous."

"Unlike Mrs. Abingdon I must earn my living. I do that by working on newspapers, as I believe you do too, Mr. Gallagher."

"Yes, and it is about newspaper work that I wanted to ask you. You know that we in New York have lost two young women to the attacks of unknown assailants. Have you encountered such crimes in Brooklyn?"

"Aside from street brawls which sometimes leave a trail of dead bodies, we have very few violent deaths in Brooklyn. I believe these two young women were followers of the arts of Eros, but that does not excuse attacks upon them. There is a prejudice against the young women who leave their rural homes and come to the city. Some people are determined to punish them in the name of protecting morality. And I am afraid that the corruption of police and magistrates may protect the perpetrators of such crimes."

"You have worked at several different newspapers both in New York and other cities. If the police are not going to find the guilty parties, perhaps the newspapers need to take up the challenge. Have you ever tried, as a newsman, to track down a criminal or discover the perpetrator of a crime? Do you think that newspapers are capable of serving justice? Should we just sit by and let innocent people be punished even when there is very little reason to think they are guilty of any crime?" Daniel's voice grew louder as he warmed to his subject.

Lawrence Abingdon leaned forward over the table. "Certainly being arrested for a crime I did not commit was a terrifying experience for me. I could feel the net being tightened around me. The Tombs is a brutal place and being kept there for any length of time could drive a man mad. It was only by a strange accident that another murder occurred while I was in prison thus leading even the police to think I might not be guilty."

"Now they have arrested a man that I know," Daniel continued. "James Jackson is a freed slave, a respectable man who has lived an honest life in this city for twenty years. Do you think anyone is going to try to prove him innocent?"

Charlotte couldn't restrain herself any longer. "I visited the Tombs with Mrs. Jackson and heard the terrible names other prisoners called out. Many people in this city believe that any colored man is capable of vicious crimes. They want to show no mercy."

"It is not so much a matter of mercy, Miss Edgerton," said Walt Whitman. "Much of the furor over what to do with freed slaves has to do with political differences. How can the Northern states possibly absorb all of the freed slaves that will come here when the vicious practice of slavery is finally abolished? Should the Africans go back to Africa to start a new country?"

"That might be the best solution," agreed Lawrence Abingdon. "God created different races and placed them in different parts of the world. Surely if He had meant us all to live together, He would not have separated the races. Black people are made differently than we are."

"You are showing your Southern roots," Whitman interjected. "You are reflecting the sentiments in your home state of Virginia. Indeed that is the Southern position in a nutshell. God made Africans as an inferior race and slavery is only a reflection of that truth. But when I listen to some of the free blacks of this city, I cannot help but believe they are far more like you and me than we might think. They pursue their dreams and seek their fortunes. Why should they not live among us in peace?"

"There are differences that any man can recognize," Lawrence Abingdon persisted. "Even as William Blake wrote about a black child:

And I am black, but oh my soul is white!
White as an angel is the English child,
But I am black, as if bereaved of light.

Not until we all stand before the gates of Heaven will all these differences disappear. It is only natural for people to seek their own kind."

"I work with a freed slave, a woman who has dreams and hopes just like mine. And the children in the school where we teach are not so different from the children I taught in Massachusetts". Charlotte spoke quietly because she was a little overawed by the conversation of the two poets, but she was determined to have her say.

"And I agree with Miss Edgerton," Daniel chimed in. "I find little more difference between the races than I see between people in my native Ireland and those here in New York. The American dream is to allow everyone to share in this new country."

"Hear, hear!" cheered Whitman. "Abingdon, you have been over-ruled. We newspapermen will seek out the truth and find justice for our freed slave and retribution for the villain who committed the crimes of which he is accused."

****

A few days later Charlotte received a note from Miss Fuller inviting her to tea, so on Sunday morning she prepared for the long trip to Horace Greeley's home at Turtle Bay. He and his wife and son lived in a country retreat several miles north of the city overlooking the East River.

The first part of the journey was on the horse-drawn cars of the Harlem Railroad, which ran up Third Avenue. Luckily the day was warm for December and peering out the dusty window, Charlotte could see the sun shining weakly through milky clouds. She got off the car at 49th Street, although she discovered it was not really a street but a narrow dirt path leading toward Turtle Bay. Sturdy linden trees lined the road and a few pines lent color to the drab brown and gray landscape.

The Greeleys' house was a rambling farmhouse, almost fifty years old and somewhat the worse for wear. A young Irish servant answered the door when Charlotte knocked and led her into the parlor. Margaret Fuller was seated at a small desk writing swiftly. She rose as Charlotte approached.

"Thank you for coming, Miss Edgerton. I trust the trip on the railroad was comfortable. It is a long way from town, but I enjoy working here in this secluded spot away from the noise and dirt of the city. Mr. and Mrs. Greeley have been kind enough to provide a room for me. I only go into the newspaper office once a week. I am sorry to say that Mrs. Greeley and her enchanting son Pinkie are not at home today. Mrs. Greeley sends her regrets and hopes she will be able to meet you another time.

"Come, let's sit in front of the fireplace and talk." She pointed toward a shabby-looking upholstered chair. Charlotte sat down gratefully.

"Now you must tell me about your school and the work Mr. Fox is doing."

"Our teaching is going well. I am very grateful to you for recommending me to the trustees at the school. Working with Mr. Fox and with Mrs. Jackson, his other teacher, has been gratifying. The students are eager to learn and a pleasure to teach. Unfortunately, the school itself is not prospering."

"Why is that? A number of prominent people support the school, I believe."

"There is some turmoil in the city these days. You have no doubt heard of the recent murders of two young women. Mrs. Jackson's husband has been arrested although he has not been charged with the killings. Because he and his wife are freed slaves, I am afraid the police are quick to assume he may be guilty. I am afraid that his misfortune has tarnished the reputation of the school. But I can assure you that both Mr. Fox and I are very sure he had nothing to do with these crimes."

Margaret Fuller lifted her lorgnette to her eyes and peered at Charlotte as she answered, "Suspicion falls so easily on the free blacks who live in the North. There are always people who will believe they are guilty of any crimes that occur. But how does this suspicion threaten the school?"

"Some of the trustees are questioning the wisdom of teaching black children. Many people, even those who are opposed to slavery, do not think the freed slaves should be encouraged to remain in New York. They are afraid the two races will never live comfortably together and wish that the Africans would be sent back to Africa.

"My hope is that if people could see the good work we are doing and how many talents the children bring to our city, there would be more support for our efforts." Charlotte leaned forward eagerly as she spoke. "I came here today to ask your advice about what we might do."

The two women stopped talking as the young maid slipped into the room with a tray of tea and biscuits. Charlotte couldn't help noticing that the teacups were chipped and the biscuits a bit stale, but she enjoyed the soothing tea as she drew a deep breath and continued to talk.

"Do you think that if the children gave a concert that would encourage support? They are all good musicians with excellent voices and an innate joy in singing. Last night I saw the Hutchison Family Singers give a concert and was impressed by the beauty of their songs and the enthusiasm of the audience."

"The Hutchison Family Singers," Margaret Fuller echoed. "They are certainly well known and successful and have done good work with their anti-slavery songs. People in this city enjoy concerts and perhaps your group of children would also arouse enthusiasm for the cause of Negro Education."

The two women talked for another hour about how Charlotte and her colleagues could plan a concert that would build goodwill for the school. "I will help to tell the public about the concert," Miss Fuller promised. "Many readers of the *Tribune* are eager supporters of both education and music. Mr. Greeley has given me the task of writing about music and other cultural events in the city. And my friend Lydia Maria Child, who is a strong advocate of abolition and education, will no doubt help by writing about your plans in her articles."

By the time she left to go back downtown, Charlotte was glowing with hope. She thought about the children at the school and their musical talents. And with Freedom Jackson to help the children learn new songs and to sing them well, surely they could impress even the sophisticated audience in New York.

"I can scarcely wait to tell Daniel about our plans," she breathed as she walked down the twilight path toward the railroad.

CHAPTER FIFTEEN

A New Music Teacher

Keep your face always toward the sunshine—and shadows will fall behind you.

Monday, December 4, 1843

On Monday morning Charlotte hoped for a chance to talk to Mr. Fox about her idea, but he had been called out of town for a few days, so she had to wait. Several days crept by while she waited impatiently for him to return. The children were as lively as ever, but Mercy Jackson looked woebegone. James Jackson was still being held in prison, although no charges had yet been brought against him. Daniel visited him and tried to get information from officials at the Hall of Justice, but he had learned nothing new. Cold weather continued and biting winds whistled around the corners of every building in the city.

Even the youngest schoolchildren knew something was wrong. A girl in Charlotte' class whispered to her

147

one morning, "My father says that Mrs. Jackson's husband is in prison and he may never get out. They say he is a murderer. They say he might kill one of us someday if he comes back to the school."

"Mr. Jackson is no murderer," Charlotte assured her. "You know he is a good man who takes care of the piano in the school. It is a mistake that he is in prison."

But Charlotte knew the poisonous gossip would continue unless something happened soon. Two of the children in her class were removed from the school. She confided to Daniel that she was afraid some of the trustees would demand that Mr. Fox ask Mercy Jackson to leave the school.

When Mr. Fox returned to the school, he asked Charlotte to come to his office. When she entered the room she noticed that Mr. Fox's usually calm brow was furrowed and he was frowning. He greeted Charlotte with his familiar patient cheer, but his heart did not seem to be in it and the tension in his face did not change.

"As you must have noted, Miss Edgerton, some parents are removing their children from our school. Many of the trustees are concerned. They say we will lose support for the school if the wife of an accused man is employed here." John Fox was clearly worried and torn about what he should do.

"But surely, Mr. Fox, James Jackson is being falsely accused and is not guilty of any crime. He and his family are suffering because of the prejudice of the police and many citizens who seize upon any opportunity to blame the freed slaves for all the trouble in the city."

"Yes, Miss Edgerton, I agree with you. I do not believe Mr. Jackson or any member of his family is a criminal, but we depend on the charity of our trustees and their friends to keep this school alive. Somehow Mr. Jackson's innocence must be proven before our school will be safe."

"We cannot control the time it will take for Mr. Jackson's trial, but perhaps there are some ways we could show the trustees and the public that the school is doing good work. If people knew about the work we do here and understood how talented the children are, perhaps they would support the school despite the unfortunate events of the past few weeks."

"How do you think that could occur?" asked Mr. Fox looking unconvinced.

"Perhaps it would help if we had the children give a public performance so people would see how hard they are working. I took the liberty of speaking to Miss Margaret Fuller a few days ago, and she encouraged me to suggest the idea to you. She agreed that the children here at the school could present a concert of American songs, somewhat like the concerts that the Hutchison Family are famous for. That might bring us much good will."

"If Miss Fuller believes we can do this, I would certainly think seriously about her advice." Mr. Fox was beginning to look a little less discouraged. "Would you prepare a plan that I could present to the trustees when we hold our next meeting. You and Mrs. Jackson will have to confer about what can be done, but it would be worthwhile to make an effort."

During the dinner break, Charlotte raised the question with Mercy. "Do you think there is any way we can encourage more people to give money to the school? Would it help if we formed the children into a singing group and gave a concert?"

Mercy frowned. "Do you think we can form these children into a singing group like the Hutchison Family?" Her face relaxed as she continued, "We could call them the Pearl Street School Singers and hire a theater for them to give their performance if we had the money. Do you think that would be possible?"

"Perhaps we couldn't hire a theater. I don't think we could raise enough money for that. But there must be someplace we could put on a performance. You should have heard the Hutchison Family harmonize their songs the other evening. It is a "true American style". That's what Mr. Whitman called it. And that style came from the minstrel shows that your son Freedom loves so much. He would know how to teach the children to sing. They enjoy singing. It's what they love most about school. Even my tiny primary children learned to sing the alphabet perfectly in almost no time. You know how easy it seems to them. You have children in your classes who are natural singers too. I've heard them."

Mercy's frown looked a little less forbidding now, although she did not give Charlotte much hope. "I will ask James what he thinks about this scheme. And I will ask Freedom whether he thinks he could teach the children. If Mr. Fox approves, I suppose we could do it. He is eager to get more support for the school."

At first no one, not even Daniel, shared Charlotte's confidence that the children could raise money on their own but gradually they came around to the idea of at least trying it. Freedom was filled with the optimism of youth and said he could form a choir in no time. He promised to come on Thursday to start the work.

Thursday came with a sprinkling of snow and a harsh wind blowing, but almost no child was absent. Mercy and Charlotte brought them all together in the larger classroom. The older boys and girls sat on benches around the walls while the younger ones sat cross-legged on the floor.

Freedom had worn his fanciest clothes—a bright blue jacket with gold button and a top hat. He started out by showing the children what they would be learning.

Camptown ladies sing a song
Doo dah Doo dah
Camptown race track's five miles long
Oh the doo dah day

Come down here with my hat caved in
Doo dah doo dah
Go back home with a pocket full of tin
Oh the doo dah day

After he finished those verses he burst into a dance, his feet flying as they tapped out the rhythm on the wooden floor. The children started clapping too and soon several of the smallest ones were up and dancing. Freedom took the hands of two of the smaller boys and encouraged them to dance along with him. Soon the three of them were tapping vigorously while the other children sang the lyrics to the song.

When the song ended, the silence echoed with the memory of it. The children looked at one another with delight. Mercy was smiling broadly and Charlotte was even more hopeful that if the children sang and danced for society people, contributions would flow in for the school.

Those happy thoughts were interrupted when the door was thrown open. Mr. Fox and two of the trustees stood in the doorway. Mr. Fox's mild voice was uncharacteristically stern, "Are you sure those are the songs and dances that you want to teach the children? Do you really think that a performance of this type will lead our friends to believe that we are providing a proper education for these young people?"

"Indeed, Mr. Fox", said Mercy speaking up boldly. "We do not intend that the children will sing the kind of songs that are used in minstrel shows. This is just a demonstration of the kind of singing of which the children are capable."

"The American style of singing with close harmonization of the voices has, I believe, become an acceptable and a popular style. I have heard the Hutchison Family Singers and they are a most respectable group. Their concerts attract a wide audience. That is the style of singing that I hope our children can achieve," Charlotte urged.

Charles Bennett Ray spoke up. "Yes, indeed, Mr. Fox, this young woman is right. As you know, I have spoken to many groups of people about some of the problems we are facing. I have made myself familiar with people throughout our city from the mansions of Washington Square to the squalid streets of Five Points. There is an extraordinary interest in the harmonies of singing groups. I believe the school could benefit from training the children to form such a group."

Rex Hamilton added his voice. "I agree with Mr. Ray. At political meetings people always enjoy music and singing. And many New Yorkers admire the Hutchison Family and their music."

"If you think so, Mr. Ray and Mr. Hamilton, then I foresee no difficulty with the other trustees over this matter. We will have to be careful to ensure that the children are dressed in becoming and appropriate clothes for a choir, but I have no doubt that Mrs. Jackson and Miss Edgerton can see to that. They can work with some of the mothers whose children attend this school."

Mr. Fox and the trustees left the room and Charlotte and Mercy breathed sighs of relief. It seemed they might be able to help the school raise money. If they did that, perhaps grateful parents and trustees would no longer talk of asking Mercy to leave the school.

"It is a good thing the trustees spoke up," said Mercy. "I am not sure Mr. Fox would have agreed with our plan on his own. Mr. Ray is a great supporter of the school and Mr. Hamilton is very persuasive and is becoming an important political figure in the city. You have heard him speak before I believe, haven't you, Freedom?"

"Only at political rallies, but I don't pay much attention to loud speeches. Politics are not for me. Yet somehow his voice sounds familiar. I wonder where I have heard that before. I don't suppose he frequents the brothels where I play the piano."

"I hardly think so," agreed Charlotte. "He is campaigning against them and trying to shut them down to make the city more pure."

Freedom stayed at the school for another hour working with the children to teach them a more decorous song. Before the day was over he had the children singing:

Swing low, sweet chariot
Coming for to carry me home,
Swing low, sweet chariot,
Coming for to carry me home.

Charlotte marveled that all of the children learned the song so easily. Their voices soared with a natural rhythm and their bodies swayed in time with the music. The students she taught in Massachusetts would never have grasped the music so easily and quickly. Surely the audience which listened to these children would understand their talents were no less than those of the white children at other schools around the city. But even as she thought that she realized how this city could bring surprises she never would have dreamed.

CHAPTER SIXTEEN

A Disappearance

I love thee to the level of every day's
Most quiet need by sun and candle light.

Sunday, December 10, 1843

Charlotte woke early on Sunday looking forward to spending some time with Daniel. She hummed as she dressed, thinking of the long walk they could take exploring parts of the city she hadn't seen yet. When she went down to breakfast, she found a note waiting for her.

Dear Miss Edgerton,

I will call on you directly after dinner on Sunday. I hope that you will enjoy taking a walk with me. Perhaps we can walk along the river and watch some of the vessels in the harbor. The sight of those ships always reminds me of our great good luck in being able to live in this city which is the center of so much business in America. In fact, it is now called

America's Empire City and Mr. Greeley has instructed us to use that language often when we are writing our news stories.

I have a little news to give you and something very special that I would like to talk about with you today, so I hope you will be willing to listen to my ramblings.

Your affectionate friend,

Daniel Gallagher

Charlotte knew that Daniel's last few days had been disappointing. He had interviewed each of the policemen and watchmen who had been at the scene of Polly's death as well as the women in the house. No one had anything new to add to what he knew about her death. Polly was a good friend to most of the women in the house and none of them wanted to say a word against her. She had no enemies they all declared. Everyone liked her. The women presented a united front against strangers asking questions,

"One after another they said they had no idea who the unidentified man who had talked to might be," Daniel had complained on Friday. "And when I asked about Polly's son and where he lived, no one was willing to tell me anything."

"Do you think we want the police to track down the boy?" Mrs. Walker had asked him. "He is six years old now and will soon be able to earn his keep. Polly's cousins will take care of him for a while longer, and I can give them some money if that is needed. Perhaps they will keep him for a few more years until he becomes old enough to work for us here. Polly would like that. But the newspapers must not get him."

Not much had changed for James Jackson either, although he had finally been charged with "Loitering with intent to cause harm." Mercy was heartbroken to have him held on such a flimsy charge, but they would have to wait now for a trial. That would take several weeks or perhaps months.

When Daniel came to the door Sunday afternoon, he was carrying a small package wrapped in paper with a carefully tied bow of blue ribbon. "I found a bakeshop that sold butterscotch candy," he said a little sheepishly. "I thought you might like some. My father used to bring home this candy occasionally when we were children. It was always Eileen's favorite. I don't know whether you are familiar with it."

"Oh, thank you! I so seldom have candy and I love butterscotch. We used to have it sometimes when I was living at Brook Farm."

Charlotte knew Daniel must have something very special to say. He looked so solemn. She tied on her bonnet quickly and they went out. The weather had turned warmer and the crowds on Broadway looked especially cheerful, smiling and laughing in the bright sunshine, but Daniel led Charlotte away from the busy street and over to the quiet pier area. Several ships rocked gently in the gray-blue water while gulls shrieked overhead and ropes squeaked each time the ships shifted in the water.

"You know I have been working hard for Mr. Greely this past year since I joined his newspaper," Daniel began. "Aside from the money I sent for Eileen's passage, I have spent almost nothing during those months. Now I finally have enough money to send my mother's passage money too. I hope to do that in a few days so she will be able to come soon, perhaps early in the spring."

"That's wonderful! You must be very proud of being able to do that. Not many men have been as successful as you have been in the newspaper business. Although are you sure your mother wants to come to a dangerous city like this with so many unsolved murders?"

"Ah, the whole world is a dangerous place! At least here we will be together to face whatever dangers come. We will get to the bottom of those unsolved murders with the help of the police. We cannot wait our whole lifetime for perfect safety. Anyway, I feel that I have done my duty. My mother and Eileen will be able to build new lives here. My other two sisters are married. They have good husbands and several children. They have some security in Ireland so they do not need my help. Now I can start to build my own life."

"And what do you intend to do with your own life, Mr. Gallagher?" Charlotte looked out at the harbor smiling because she thought she knew the answer to her question.

"I suspect you know very well what I want to say, Miss Edgerton. Now that I have completed my duty to bring my sister and mother here to America and have a job that enables me to live with a certain amount of comfort, I believe that I can take on the responsibility of a wife." Daniel paused as though he found it difficult to speak. "We have always spoken honestly with one another, so I hope you will not object to my straightforward words. Will you become my wife?"

Charlotte had no doubt about what her answer would be, but she could not resist teasing Daniel a little. "You are a poet, Mr. Gallagher, but you have not spoken very poetically."

"I am afraid my poetry is not good enough to tell you all that is in my heart. The best I can do is to repeat the poem I sent to you last winter when I arrived in New York. It is still true.

Sad the bird that sings alone,
Flies to wilds, unseen to languish,
Pours, unheard, the ceaseless moan,
And wastes on desert air its anguish!

I am still lonely. I am lonely whenever I am away from you. Would you join your life with mine? We will not be rich, but I believe we can build a life for ourselves and, with God's help, our children. That will be the happiest life I can imagine. Having you by my side would change the world for me."

Charlotte turned toward him blushing and smiling. "Of course I will marry you, Daniel Gallagher. You are the only man I have ever met who made me think about marriage. Despite the differences in our backgrounds, despite the fact that we come from different countries, I believe our hearts are in tune. We belong together and I certainly promise to become your wife."

"I have not bought a new ring for you to wear to commemorate our betrothal," Daniel said, "but I would like to give you this ring my father received from his great leader, Wolfe Tone, when he fought for Ireland many years ago. My father gave it to me just before he died and I have kept it ever since. It is far too large for you to wear on your finger, but perhaps you could wear it on a chain around your neck."

For an hour after that they walked up and down the dirty, littered street along the piers. They scarcely saw the garbage scattered on the muddy pavement or smelled the fish heads being scavenged by aggressive pigs and snarling dogs. They were busy talking about when Charlotte would be ready to be married. Early spring seemed best. By that time Daniel's mother would probably be there for the ceremony.

"I must speak to Mr. Fox about continuing my teaching," Charlotte insisted. "I am not willing to give that up, and we can use the extra money if we are to find a new place to live."

"Will the school keep a married woman as a teacher?" Daniel asked.

"They allow Mrs. Jackson to teach, so how can they deny me the same right? The Pearl Street School is not one of your fancy society schools. It must take the people who are willing to teach there for very small pay."

When Daniel suggested they walk up to the Van Pelt's house and tell Eileen the great news, Charlotte was happy to go. The city looked brighter than it ever had before. Both she and Daniel were looking forward to continuing to do the work they loved. They would not have an easy life, but the possibilities seemed endless. Charlotte would not be surprised if Daniel decided to start his own newspaper some day and then perhaps she could write articles about the important issues of the times. And eventually their children would work around them—the future was vague and hazy, but it was bright and sunny in Charlotte's imagination.

When they reached Washington Square they joined other strollers enjoying the unusually warm weather. Houses here were tall and gray with forbidding stoops of granite. The windows stretched so tall that Charlotte knew they must go from the floor almost to the ceiling in the parlor rooms. Beyond the windows she could glimpse velvet drapes and dark, heavy furniture. They could see servants carrying tea trays in many of the rooms and fires being lit in the massive marble fireplaces.

When they reached the Van Pelt house, they walked around to the servants' entrance and went through the pantry to the kitchen. Both the cook and Molly, the second housemaid, recognized Daniel and Charlotte, but to their surprise, there was no cheerful greeting.

"Oh, Mr. Gallagher, I was about to send a note to you" said the cook. "I am sure I do not know where your sister could have disappeared to."

"Disappeared?" Daniel's face paled. "How could she have disappeared?"

"Indeed I don't know," said Molly. "Yesterday was her half day and she said she was going to visit a friend of hers. When she wasn't back by bedtime, I thought she might be staying late with her friend. And when she wasn't in her bed this morning, I decided she must have been afraid to come home so late. I said to myself that she was probably spending the night with her friend."

"There was no need for her to be so afraid of me," said the cook. "Of course I lock the door at night. It is my duty to see that the maids don't stray outside or have young men come in to see them. But I would have opened the door for Eileen if she had wakened me. The day was quiet. I went out myself to see my sister and did not notice that Eileen had not returned by evening."

"On Sunday morning the Van Pelts encourage all of us to go to church, so Eileen was not missed" continued Molly. "But now Mr. Van Pelt will expect all of us to attend the afternoon prayers he has for all of the family and staff. Her absence will be noticed."

The glow the day had brought faded abruptly as Daniel and Charlotte considered what might have happened. They decided to retrace the route Eileen would have taken if she had been walking to Thomas Street to visit Charlotte or Daniel. Perhaps there was something along the way that would explain the mystery.

They walked slowly across Washington Square wondering where to start. At the other side, where traffic was busiest, they saw a carriage stop and a woman step out. Charlotte caught her breath, "Daniel, there she is! What is she doing in that carriage?"

The carriage drove away and the woman walked hurriedly toward the Van Pelt's side of the Square. Daniel soon confronted her. "Eileen, what is going on? We were told you had disappeared. Where have you been?"

"I must get back to the house as quickly as possible," Eileen insisted. "It is all a mistake. I am afraid I made a terrible mistake, but I will be safe now if Mrs. Van Pelt does not see me come in."

CHAPTER SEVENTEEN

Trust and Suspicion

He'll come home, he'll not forget me, for his word is always true.

Monday, December 11, 1843

Eileen brushed past Charlotte and Daniel and disappeared into the servant's entrance. Charlotte's emotions were in turmoil. She and Daniel had been in a daze of happiness when they walked along the waterfront planning their future. Then came the terror of Eileen's disappearance and now the shock of her abrupt reappearance. The two of them walked slowly back toward Thomas Street not saying anything. What was there to say?

Whatever had happened to Eileen overnight could not have been good. If she was lucky Mrs. Van Pelt would never know about her absence. How would she explain it to Cook and to Molly? Charlotte knew Eileen had no close friends in New York that she could spend the night with. Where does a young woman go at night in the city? Charlotte could not think of any respectable place, but she hesitated to say that to Daniel.

With a scowl on his face, Daniel strode along. He said nothing until they were almost at Charlotte's boarding house. Then he finally spoke, "I thought I was protecting Eileen here in New York. My mother trusted me to take care of her and be sure she was safe. She is very young and knows nothing about city life. Unlike you, Charlotte, she has never had to make her way in the world alone."

"You did take care of her, Daniel. You helped her find the position with Mrs. Van Pelt, who is a most respectable woman. You are lucky Mr. Greeley was willing to write a letter for Eileen and vouch that she came from an honest, hard-working family. She has to learn to encounter people outside of the family and become accustomed to city life. There is no better place for her to do that than in the Van Pelt household."

"But how was she enticed to leave the house and to stay out all night? There was a man in that carriage, Charlotte. Why would she be sharing a carriage with a strange man? What kind of evil has she been led into?"

"Don't be so melodramatic! It may be no evil at all. Perhaps it was just an innocent mistake that led to her spending a night outside of the house. You must talk to her and find out what actually happened. I'm sure you will feel better when you hear the whole story."

"I don't want to play the heavy-handed brother rushing in to chastise his little sister. I'm afraid I've done that too often. Eileen is the youngest in the family and she was always a lively, spirited girl. After my father died, my mother expected me to take his place in making sure Eileen did not become wild or get herself into trouble.

"She told me she wasn't sure she wanted to take my money to come to America because she wanted to be independent and come on her own. That was impossible of course. There was no money to be had for her in Ireland. But you should have heard her telling me how she was going to repay me for her passage and never be a debtor to me. She always said 'Don't treat me like a baby, Daniel, you are not my father.' She would not welcome my questions now."

"Then let me talk to her. After we are married she will truly be my sister. Perhaps it will be easier for her to tell me what happened."

On Monday afternoon after classes were over, Charlotte walked to the Van Pelt house. When she knocked on the door, Molly opened it and seemed glad to see Charlotte. She spoke urgently.

"Eileen was very lucky yesterday. She took part in the afternoon prayers and helped serve the evening meal as cool as could be. None of the Van Pelts knew she had been out overnight, I'm sure. Mrs. Van Pelt is very strict about the behavior of her staff. She doesn't like us to go to theaters, much less taverns. Eileen is lucky she has friends to stay with because otherwise Mrs. Van Pelt might have thought she was carousing in some sporting house or wandering the streets."

"Yes, Eileen is very lucky. Her brother and I were worried when we discovered she had not been here, but I am sure that such a mistake will not happen again. It's so easy for people to forget the time when they are with friends."

The afternoon was a quiet time and Eileen was free to visit with Charlotte until it was time to serve supper to the family. The two of them were able to talk in a quiet corner of the servants' parlor.

"I am very happy you are going to be my sister, Charlotte. It is all right to call you Charlotte now, isn't it? Daniel has told us so much about you. He loves you very much and I know he has been looking forward to being able to ask you to marry him."

"Yes, and I am equally happy to be asked," Charlotte assured her. "You and I will be the best of friends now that we are all to be one family."

But after the excited talk about the wedding plans, Charlotte knew she must ask Eileen about her adventure. The answer she received was not what she had hoped.

"You may not understand why I would do this, Charlotte, but that is because you do not know Charles."

"Who is Charles?"

"Charles Van Pelt. He is the youngest son in the Van Pelt family. He has been very kind to me ever since I came here. One day when I was dusting the mantel in the library and was having trouble reaching the tall candlesticks, he came over and lifted one down for me.

"After that he would often help me when he saw me working in one of the rooms. He asked me where I came from and how long I had been in New York. And he told me I was the prettiest maid who had ever come to this house."

"And I suppose he tried to kiss you," Charlotte interrupted.

"Well, yes he did, after a while. But he always kissed me very respectfully and he kept his hands to himself."

"Respectful, was he?" Charlotte laughed. "And did he get down on one knee and beg you to favor him with a kiss."

"Don't be silly, Charlotte. We never had more than a minute or two alone and there was no time for that. But he wanted to be my friend. He asked about my family and told me about places I should visit on my days off. Then last Saturday morning he came into the parlor when I was dusting and asked if I'd like to take a trip on a ferry and visit one of the prettiest spots I'd ever seen. He told me we could be back in plenty of time because we had all afternoon."

"And where was this lovely spot?"

"He said it was a town called Jamaica. Just a short ride from the ferry pier in Brooklyn."

"I don't know of Jamaica. Is that on Long Island?"

"Yes, and it is a lively place. We took the ferry across to Brooklyn. Oh, it was such fun watching the waves and seeing the shore come close." Eileen's eyes shone when she talked about it. "In Jamaica there is a racetrack that many people visit. It was so exciting! We stopped at an inn and had a delicious meal, but the cooking took a long time and by the time we had eaten it was dark. I hadn't even noticed how dark it was getting."

"You didn't stay at the inn overnight with him?" Charlotte asked. The girl's reputation would be ruined if people found she had spent the night at an inn with a man. Daniel would be angry and worried.

"Yes, I did," said Eileen defiantly. "Charles was so nice to me. He persuaded me that it would be dangerous to try to ride back to Brooklyn in the dark. And the ferry closes at sundown."

"Did he get you a room of your own? That's what a gentleman would have done."

"I don't think there were enough rooms. Anyway, Charles took me upstairs to a room and we sat by the fire and talked. And he asked the landlord to bring us some wine. And he was so kind and told me I was the prettiest girl he had ever seen. And he kissed me and then…well. I'm sure he wants to marry me." Her voice trailed off.

"On the drive back this morning he said we must tell no one about what we had done because his parents would be angry. But when the time comes he will tell them and then I am sure we will get married. Daniel says that in America men and women can marry whomever they choose. The Van Pelts are not lords or ladies. They are Americans just like everyone else."

"The Van Pelts are not just like everyone else. Mr. Van Pelt is a wealthy merchant and his sons will be very wealthy too. And wealthy men do not marry housemaids. Not even in America. You should leave this house and find another position. If anything happens and Mrs. Van Pelt finds out about this she will never write a reference for you. You will have to leave in disgrace and then what will you do?"

"You wait and see," Eileen persisted. "It will not be like that. Charles loves me and he will marry me when he has found the right time to tell his father about us. Don't tell Daniel. He will think he has to fight with Charles to protect my honor. Then he would be in trouble too. Just you wait! It will be all right. You will see. Promise me you won't tell Daniel. Please, Charlotte, please!"

"I can't keep secrets from Daniel, especially not secrets about you, Eileen. Don't ask me to do that."

"Just wait for a few weeks then," Eileen pleaded. "Wait until after Christmas. I am sure Charles will say something about marriage soon. Then we can tell Daniel."

Charlotte was despondent as she walked back to the boarding house. She hated not telling Daniel all that Eileen had told her, but she was afraid he would get himself into trouble. Men were so quick to think they have to act like knights in armor to protect their sisters, wives and mothers, but that kind of behavior usually led to more trouble. Surely Charles Van Pelt had no intention of marrying Eileen and the sooner she learned that the better. Then this one slip might be forgotten. If nothing came of it Eileen would learn a bitter lesson, but she would be better off for it. Despite what preachers said about a woman's virtue being fragile, many a woman had not fallen irretrievably into a life of sin and suffering after just one mistake.

Daniel's job was going well, but he needed to establish himself. His reputation would be tarnished if Mr. Greeley or others learned about Eileen's indiscretion. No sense asking for trouble. Charlotte decided she would keep her promise to Eileen and not tell Daniel the full story until after Christmas. No matter what happened she would tell him before they got married. They must have no secrets when they entered marriage.

Meanwhile there were other problems to worry about. James Jackson was still in prison. Mercy Jackson might lose her job if the mystery of the two murders was not solved. And nothing would strengthen Daniel's job prospects more than discovering the culprit and bringing him to the police.

CHAPTER EIGHTEEN

Fear Visits Chamber Street

And why beholdest thou the mote that is in thy brother's eye, but considerest not the beam that is in thine own eye?

Wednesday, December 13, 1843

A soft snow was falling outside and the gentlemen arriving at Alice Taylor's well-known establishment on Chamber Street shook snowflakes off their overcoats as they entered. It was an evening when a man needed a warm fire and some music to relax after a day's work. And the presence of lovely, friendly young ladies added to the charm. Mrs. Taylor made sure that champagne and whiskey were available for guests and Freedom Jackson played cheerful tunes on the piano.

Lawrence Abingdon leaned back in his chair and listened as a black-haired girl in a dress bright with stripes of gray and scarlet sang to the guests:

I dreamt I dwelt in marble halls
With vassals and serfs at my side.
And of all who assembled within those walls
That I was the hope and the pride.

It was a familiar tune and Lawrence listened peacefully. He had avoided going to the brothels after Susan died, but it was time to join again in the friendly pastimes of that marked New York. Grief was not meant to last forever and poor Susan was, one hoped, enjoying the pleasures of paradise. Surely she had earned herself a place there even though her life had not been exemplary.

"Don't you have any livelier music?" called one of the men who clutched his third glass of wine and waved it toward Freedom. "What about a minstrel tune?"

Obligingly Freedom swung into the quick rhythm of Camptown Races and most of the assembled group sang the rollicking words with him.

Come down here with my hat caved in
Doo dah doo dah
Go back home with a pocket full of tin
Oh the doo dah day
Goin' to run all night
Goin' to run all day
I'll bet my money on the bobtail nag
Somebody bet on the bay

"Is that lively enough for you Mr. Williams?" Freedom asked the man who had requested a lively tune.

"Yes indeed," the man answered, gulping down the last of his wine as he stood up and put his arm around the waist of one of the women. He bowed slightly to the audience as he led her up to the second floor.

Mrs. Taylor turned to Lawrence. "Would you read one of your poems to us, Mr. Abingdon?" she asked.

"I am writing a new poem called "The Dream". Alas, it is not finished yet, but I can give you the opening verses. I am sure we have all felt these sentiments." His voice was a smooth baritone. Freedom turned his piano stool around so he could listen closely."

In visions of the dark night
I have dreamed of joy departed-
But a waking dream of life and light
Hath left me broken-hearted.

Ah! what is not a dream by day
To him whose eyes are cast
On things around him with a ray
Turned back upon the past?

While Abingdon was reading, a group of three men came in. They were more in the mood for cheerful chatter than for poetry, so the talk soon turned to more worldly subjects. Lawrence moved to a corner of the room, sat in his favorite chair and pulled out a small notebook to make notes upon his thoughts. He was determined to finish this poem.

Freedom was asked to dance and he obliged with one of his lively tap dances. All eyes were turned on him, but he noticed another man come in from outside, slip off his coat and stand in the doorway of the parlor. Freedom finished his dance and took a few bows, noticing the smiles on everyone's face except for the newcomer, a tall, robust man with a dark beard who lingered in the hall frowning as he looked around the room.

As the unknown man glowered around the room, a tall young woman in a crimson dress approached him. "You need cheering up, sir. Can I get you a glass of champagne?"

The man murmured an acceptance and a glass of champagne was soon produced. By this time the parlor chairs were filled, so the man stood in the doorway, looking thoughtfully around at the women in the room as he drank his wine.

"Come sir, would you like to suggest a song," Mrs. Taylor asked him. "You are a newcomer to our circle and we would like to welcome you."

The man bowed, "John Smith at your service, ma'am. Yes, I'll have a song. Perhaps it is time for a hymn—a good old fashioned hymn like Isaac Watts' song about purity."

There was silence for a moment as Mrs. Taylor and the other women stared at the newcomer.

"I'm afraid I don't know that song," stammered Freedom.

"Here is how it goes," Mr. Smith announced and proceeded to speak in a firm voice:

Blest are the pure, whose hearts are clean,

Who never tread the ways of sin;
With endless pleasures they shall see
A God of spotless purity.

Blest are the men of peaceful life,
Who quench the coals of growing strife,
They shall be called the heirs of bliss,
The sons of God, the God of peace.

"Come, come, sir," Lawrence Abington's voice broke the silence that followed. "I am sure we can all follow our own hearts and we will be judged only by God," he said. "There is no need for preaching here. Let us enjoy our time among friends."

Abington's speech was followed by a general murmur of approval. The young woman in scarlet turned away from the stranger and turned to smile at others. Soon the audience started to disappear. Most of the men slipped upstairs with one of the women, but some made their way out onto the snowy street. Lawrence Abingdon was one of the last to leave. He slowly tucked his notebook into his pocket as he started up and looked around absent-mindedly as though he had forgotten he was part of a group. When he saw the empty chairs, he found his overcoat, wrapped a long scarf around his neck and walked out onto the chilly street.

Freedom was eager to get home before the snow grew worse. He took the coins Mrs. Taylor had given him, added a few that had been tossed onto the piano by some of the gentlemen, and made his way out. The street was quiet and the house behind him even more silent as he made his way down the snowy street. Not until almost midnight did Mrs. Taylor lock and bolt the door leaving only the women of the house and a few of their special guests who had arranged to spent the night inside.

******

Morning brought brilliant sunshine. The snow had stopped and even dirty, muddy Chambers Street looked clean in the new snow. But none of the women of the house saw the pristine streets of early morning. By the time they got up and looked out of their windows the snow had been churned by buggy wheels and horses' hooves. A few dogs scavenged through the snow looking for scraps of food and peddlers urged their tired old nags along while calling out "Milk, fresh milk for sale".

In Mrs. Taylor's house, the cook had made porridge and cooked bacon. The smell of fresh-baked bread filled the kitchen. The women of the house came to breakfast in their wrappers and with their hair uncombed. They good-naturedly teased one another and planned shopping trips.

"Where is Beatrice?" asked Mrs. Taylor. "Who was that John Smith who came in last night? I've never seen that man before and I don't think I want to see him again."

"Nor have I," Mary Abbot remarked. "Beatrice has left, I think. She told me yesterday that she was going to visit her son in Brooklyn this morning. This surely is a cold day for a visit. I hope the river isn't frozen. One time…"

She broke off as she heard a shout from the kitchen. The cook and her young son soon burst into the room. The boy was crying. "I didn't do nothing! I went outside to get some wood for the fire and there was Miss Clark lying on the ground. She's dead! I know she's dead!"

The women rushed to the back door where they found Beatrice Clark lying, half-covered with snow already. Within a few minutes the cook's young son was sent off to tell the police office at the Tombs about what had happened. In less than an hour a policeman was at Mrs. Taylor's house and word of another murder had spread to several newspaper offices. The mid-morning quiet on Chambers Street disappeared as a crowd of spectators gathered around the house. Daniel was among them.

Denied entry into the house, Daniel began questioning the spectators who were gathering around the house. Few of them knew anything, but Daniel was determined to find someone who did, so he went around to the back of the house and entered through the kitchen door. The cook had been banished to the kitchen, and was unhappy at not seeing what was going on. When Daniel arrived she welcomed him eagerly. "Tell me are the police here? What are they asking about? Is there a big crowd?"

"The crowd is not so big," Daniel answered. "The police are questioning Mrs. Taylor and the women about everything that happened last night and this morning. Were you here last night? Did anything unusual happen?"

"Unusual? Not that I heard. There was the usual singing and people coming in and out. Mrs. Taylor kept us busy didn't she?" Her eyes turned toward her son. "Tom and myself were working all the evening keeping up with them."

"I saw the dancing too," boasted Tom, who could scarcely have been more than ten years old. "I saw the colored man dancing and everyone was clapping. And then that other man read a poem that didn't say much. But mostly I liked the singing."

"Who was the man who did the dancing?"

"Freedom his name is," said the cook. "Freedom Jackson. He comes here often to play tunes or to dance. Mrs. Taylor is generous with the money. Her being partly colored herself she would be, wouldn't she? And his father tunes the piano."

Mrs. Taylor entered the kitchen, putting an end to the conversation, but at least Daniel had a good idea of where he could discover more information about what had occurred on the evening before the murder. He would walk over to the Pearl Street School and ask to see Mercy Jackson and perhaps her son too.

CHAPTER NINETEEN

Secrets of the Night

Hope is the thing with feathers
That perches in the soul.

Thursday, December 14, 1843

Daniel pushed his way through the crowd still loitering around the brothel and walked to the Pearl Street School to look for Freedom. Luck was against him. The building was quiet with no strains of music coming from either classroom. From Charlotte's room, Daniel could hear the high-pitched voices of children reciting alphabet rhymes. After a brief hesitation, he knocked softly on the door.

Charlotte frowned when she saw him and told him in a brief whisper that Freedom was coming after the dinner break to teach the children more songs. She gasped when Daniel just as quietly whispered to her that there had been another suspicious death. He decided to wait for Freedom and sat down on a chair in the hall to write his story:

Citizens of this city have found they are being haunted by a growing evil among us. Another well-known lady of the night has been found dead. Could she have been another victim of the same cold blooded killer who has struck before? That is the question that people are asking now. Beatrice Clark was well-known for her elegant gowns and especially for her charming hats. She was a milliner who has made hats for some of the most fashionable women in this city, but last night she met a cruel fate.

The police are investigating all the people present last night at an impromptu concert in the Chambers Street residence where Beatrice Clark lived. Her death, coming as it does on the heels of two other shocking murders, has made our officials determined to find the vicious person behind this attack. It is difficult to believe that these young women had enemies. A jealous suitor may be guilty of one murder, but no one can believe that three killings in a row are all the work of jealous suitors. Some evil force is skulking around our streets and striking down vulnerable women. Surely this proves, even if nothing else does, the importance of increasing our police force from a paltry group of a dozen or so civilian police into a truly professional corps of trained men.

The door of Charlotte's classroom finally opened and the children scampered out for their dinner break. Daniel walked to the door of the classroom to watch Charlotte clean the last of the slates and arrange them on the long benches where the children sat. Together they went into the small kitchen area where she and Mercy usually ate their dinner. Charlotte had brought some porridge and sliced meat from her breakfast and Daniel had bought some bread and cheese from the bakeshop on his way to the school. They joined Mercy Jackson at the kitchen table to eat.

"At least they can't blame my husband for this," Mercy Jackson exclaimed when Daniel told them the news. "That is one blessing, although the Lord doesn't seem to be scattering many other blessings around this city, does He?"

"Are all of these deaths connected?" asked Charlotte. "How does anyone know whether they are?"

"Well, I've lived in this city for twenty years," Mercy answered. "I've never heard of this kind of killing going on. There was one murder in a brothel about five years ago, but that was a case of jealousy and the man was quickly caught. But never one death after another! That has never happened."

"Mrs. Taylor told me she thought there was a madman on the loose." Daniel remembered the woman's frightened face when she spoke about it. "And women who live the way Beatrice Clark and the other victims did have no way to protect themselves. We need a better police force in this city. If sporting girls can be killed so easily, life will become dangerous for any woman who is on the street after dark."

"Why did you come over here to tell us this in the middle of the day?" Charlotte finally asked.

"I was looking for Freedom. The cook's boy said he was at the brothel last night singing and dancing. Does he do that often?"

"He has made up his mind to make a living by his music," his mother said. "He performs wherever he gets a chance. It helps us pay the bills and it could lead to a good job for him. Musicians can't be fussy about where they perform. By why isn't he here now? The music lesson should begin soon. What if the police have picked him up! Where can he be?"

That question was answered when Freedom walked in the door. As Daniel watched his loose-limbed grace and saw he cheerful face, he looked so young and guileless it was hard to imagine anyone would suspect him of crime. His face darkened when he sat down and heard what they were talking about.

"Yes, I was at Mrs. Taylor's house last night," he admitted. "I don't like to talk about it here because Mr. Fox and the trustees are so opposed to the brothels. But where else could I play my music and earn some money? There aren't many people willing to give a colored boy a job."

"Best you don't talk about it," Mercy added. "Your mother may lose her job if the school finds out the kind of work you do and where you do it. Some of the trustees are hell bent on getting all the brothels closed. I wouldn't want them to think that one of the teachers was supporting that kind of sinful activity."

"Did anything unusual happen while you were at the house last night?" Daniel asked.

"There was one peculiar thing. A stranger came into the house and, when Mrs. Taylor asked him to suggest a song, he started reciting some poem about purity. It sounded odd in that place. But Mr. Abingdon, he just said straight out that no one should say poems like that. People had a right to decide what to do; that's what Mr. Abingdon said."

"Mrs. Taylor's house isn't illegal," said Charlotte. "I feel sorry for women who have to live that way, but the police don't arrest anyone unless they are making a public nuisance."

"Her house and all the others will be illegal if some people get their way," muttered Freedom. "But if they close down all the bawdy houses where will people go to have a lively night out? All the young men and women— how can they enjoy themselves? Boarding houses don't even let men and women talk together. Everyone has to be so stiff and proper. Young people need to be able to go someplace to have fun."

The children were trooping back from their dinners, so the conversation had to end. The two women went back into their classrooms to prepare for the music lesson. Daniel tried to find out more about the night before. "Did you recognize the people there? Do the same men come every time you are entertaining or are there many strangers?"

"I know all of the women because I've been going there for months. Some of them have friends who come just about every night. I see them all the time. Beatrice has a special friend who's usually enjoying the music. Gives me two-bits sometimes too. But I didn't see him last night. Mr. Abingdon was there. You know him, the same man who knows Rowena Scott and was such a friend of Susan Jones."

"Yes, you mentioned that Lawrence Abingdon was there." Daniel wondered about this. What had happened to all his grief over Susan if he was out so soon enjoying a party? But still, he couldn't have had anything to do with the murder. He had been in prison when Polly died.

"Yeah, he was there all evening. He was reading some of his poetry as usual. Even after almost everyone else had gone upstairs he was sitting in the corner writing in his notebook. He was there when I left."

"But most of the men you didn't know?"

"Some of them looked familiar, but I don't always hear their names. And I don't know if they are using their real names. There was a Mr. Smith there—Mr. John Smith. I heard his name, but I had never seen him before. He was real friendly with Beatrice. She was kind of welcoming him, but she didn't like the poem he read."

Daniel hadn't learned as much as he had hoped. He knew what Freedom said was true. Men who went to brothels often used false names. John Smith—wouldn't you think someone could come up with a name that sounded a little more real?

Freedom went into the classroom to work with the students and soon the strains of "Oh, Susannah, don't you cry for me…" came floating through the hall. The office door opened and Mr. Fox came out with a man Daniel recognized one of them as the mayoral candidate, Rex Hamilton.

"You are the young reporter who interviewed me for Mr. Greeley's *Tribune*, aren't you?" asked Rex Hamilton. He did not wait for an answer. "Fine article you wrote. I hope your paper will be supporting my campaign for mayor."

He turned to the man at his side, "I have been talking to Mr. Fox about how we can raise money to keep up his good work at the school. Many of the leading citizens in our city support this school."

"Yes," Mr. Fox joined in. "The terrible affair about Mr. Jackson and his connection with the school has not worked well for us. Mrs. Jackson has been an asset to the school, but it is difficult to avoid criticism when crime comes so close to our doors."

"Have you gentlemen heard that there has been yet another apparent murder?" Daniel asked. "A woman named Beatrice Clark was found dead just outside Mrs. Taylor's house on Chambers Street."

"Another murder? This is a blot upon our city," Rex Hamilton sounded as though he was addressing a political meeting. "Our city cannot endure these dens of sin and iniquity in our midst. We must find a way to close down all the brothels in the city. Women should lead sheltered lives in their own homes, taking care of their husband and children. The forward young women who stroll about our streets in their fancy dresses cause scandal in our neighborhoods. Women cannot take care of themselves and their children without the strength of a man behind them. We must put an end to this unnatural life."

"May I quote you on that?" Daniel asked eagerly. "Our readers will be glad to hear the opinion of one of our political leaders on this matter." Rex Hamilton quickly agreed.

John Fox was more interested in the new crime. "Has anyone suggested who might be responsible for the death of Beatrice Clark? As I understand it, Mr. Jackson is still being held, so he certainly cannot be accused of this death."

"Certainly not," Daniel assured him. "It does not seem that anyone connected to this school could be threatened." He said nothing about the fact that Freedom Jackson had been in the house the night before. After Mr. Hamilton's explosive remarks, he did not want to mention the boy's activities. Surely not even Mr. Hamilton would suggest that a young boy like Freedom might be guilty of such terrible crimes.

Mr. Fox went back to his office and Daniel pulled out his notebook to write down Rex Hamilton's words. A statement from him would strengthen Daniel's article, although it would not help to solve the crime.

As he stood in the hallway writing, Daniel looked up to see Freedom Jackson standing at the door of the classroom watching him.

"Did you hear our conversation?" Daniel asked.

"I heard part of it. That Mr. Hamilton sure has a loud voice, doesn't he, even when he's not making a speech? It reminds me of something but I'm not sure where I heard it before."

CHAPTER TWENTY

Trouble in Pearl Street

Courage is resistance to fear, mastery of fear, not absence of fear.

Thursday, December 14, 1843

Daniel soon left to return to the *Tribune* office and Freedom started rehearsing the children for their concert. Mr. Fox too was leaving early that day to speak to a Dorcas Society meeting at a nearby church and ask the women for help in obtaining warm clothing for students. After the men left, Mercy and Charlotte combined their two classes in the larger classroom where all the children could practice the songs they planned to sing at the New Year concert. They struggled to learn the odd Scottish words of Robert Burn's song.

> *Should old acquaintance be forgot,*
> *and never brought to mind ?*
> *Should old acquaintance be forgot,*
> *and old lang syne ?*

For auld lang syne, my dear,
for auld lang syne,
we'll take a cup of kindness yet,
for auld lang syne.

The song brought Charlotte memories of her childhood in England. Her father used to sing that song at family gatherings at the end of each year. That was during the happy years before the crops had begun to fail and the farmers brought in the harvesting machines that put so many men out of work. The years when her mother and father could laugh and sing in the evening— when they had wood to put in the fire and food to make a meal. Later came the wretched years when they seemed to live on half-frozen turnips and watery porridge, when her mother refused her own food so the little ones could be fed. That was when Charlotte knew she would have to leave and try her luck in America. She never regretted leaving, but sometimes the sound of music she had heard so long ago brought tears to her eyes and she ached to hear her father's hearty voice singing "we'll take a cup of kindness yet, for auld lang syne".

They were all so busy singing that no one heard the outside door open and they were surprised when the classroom door opened and James Jackson entered. His wife flew to him and seized his hands.

"Oh, they have released you. Praise the Lord! We are so glad to have you here."

"Yes, the policeman said there had been another murder, which convinced the magistrate that I could not have been responsible for the first two. The guard just unlocked the door and told me to go home. He said they didn't want to spend any more money feeding me." He scoffed. "Not that they ever gave me more than a half-penny worth of food down there."

Freedom's young face was beaming. He shook his father's hand and clapped him on the shoulder. "It has been so long. Now you will be here to celebrate Christmas with us and to welcome in the New Year."

A loud noise outside startled them. It sounded as though someone had thrown a rock at the door of the school. Mr. Jackson looked out the window with a worried frown. "There may be trouble. When I left the prison, someone of the men in the crowd outside the Tombs called out 'There he goes the black killer of white women. He should be strung up. Let's tar and feather him'."

"But they didn't hurt you?" Mercy interrupted.

"No, the guard at the doorway chased the scoundrels away and I hurried to lose myself in the crowd on Broadway. But when I got a few blocks away I saw a couple of the same men again and it looks as though they followed me here. Maybe Mr. Fox can get rid of them."

"Mr. Fox has left already," Charlotte told James Jackson. "We are the only people here, so we shall have to take care of those ruffians ourselves. And we must protect the children."

Charlotte looked around at the small group in the hall—two women, an elderly man and a young boy. They were hardly likely to scare a group of hooligans. The noise outside was growing louder as though others were joining the few who had followed Mr. Jackson to the school. More rocks came clattering onto the door and then the sound of footsteps and scuffling on the steps outside.

Charlotte went to the window and looked out carefully, standing as far to the side as she could. It was growing dark. About twenty men were gathered in front of the school. They clustered in small groups on the sidewalk, talking to each other, trying to work up courage perhaps to storm the school.

"We protect our womenfolk!" shouted a loud voice. "Black men should go back to Africa. We don't want them here."

"If the police won't punish murderers, we'll do it ourselves," shouted another man.

"My father is no murderer," muttered Freedom. "I'm going to go out and fight those men."

"There are twenty of them and one of you. What chance would you have?" his father retorted. "Fighting without a chance of winning is no sort of bravery. It's just foolishness."

"We should sing!" exclaimed Charlotte. "They don't know how few people we have here. The children can all sing loudly. If they think we have a whole crowd, maybe they will go away."

"What's the loudest song you've rehearsed?" asked Mr. Jackson.

"Gospel Train's A'Coming. Let's sing that." Freedom didn't wait for an answer. He gathered the biggest children today and told them to stand right behind the door and sing as loud as ever they could. His father gestured toward Mercy and Charlotte and they gathered the smaller children together and placed them behind the others. Freedom sounded a note and the song began.

The gospel train is coming,
I hear it just at hand,
I hear the car wheels moving,
And rumbling thro' the land.
Get on board, children,
Get on board, children,
Get on board, children,
For there's room for many a more.

When they had finished one verse they started another. Charlotte peeked out the window and saw the leader of the group outside step back a few paces and look around uncertainly.

"Columbia the Gem of the Ocean" Charlotte called out excitedly and Freedom led the children in singing:

O Columbia! the gem of the ocean,
The home of the brave and the free,
The shrine of each patriot's devotion,
A world offers homage to thee;
Thy mandates make heroes assemble,
When Liberty's form stands in view;
Thy banners make tyranny tremble,
When borne by the red, white, and blue.

When borne by the red, white, and blue,
When borne by the red, white, and blue,
Thy banners make tyranny tremble,
When borne by the red, white and blue.

Both James Jackson and Freedom had deep, strong voices that rang out clear and loud. All of the children sang well and loudly too. They were used to full-throated singing in church and well accustomed to letting out all the stops. Charlotte's heart beat faster as she felt the power of their massed voices and she sang louder and stronger than she ever had before.

Thy banners make tyranny tremble,
When borne by the red, white, and blue.
When borne by the red, white, and blue,
When borne by the red, white, and blue,
Thy banners make tyranny tremble,
When borne by the red, white and blue.

"That ought to make them tremble. They will think there are fifty of us here," she said to the group.

Mercy was standing at the side of the window now. It was almost completely dark now, but black figures against the snow were still visible. "They are turning away," she whispered. "The people at the back have slipped off. Listen! No one is calling out anything anymore. I think they believe they are outnumbered."

Only one man was left standing outside of the school. He held a flaming torch in his hand and raised his arm as though he was going to hurl it at the door of the school. Charlotte ran to the door and started to loosen the bolt.

"Don't open the door!" wailed Mercy. "He'll come storming in."

"I'll go," James Jackson said firmly. "This is a job for a man."

"No." Charlotte was determined. "Seeing black faces will only inflame him more. If he sees me, he'll be ashamed to hurt me." Without waiting for an answer, she opened the door and moved out onto the top step.

"What kind of man are you to threaten defenseless women and children? Don't you read your Bible? 'Vengeance is mine' sayeth the Lord' Only cowards skulk about in the night and take the law into their own hands. Let the law take its course. Crimes are not solved by fire and violence." Her voice was so strong and forceful that she scarcely recognized it.

"I didn't know there was a white woman in there," was the shamefaced answer. "I'm an honest man and I don't hurt women. But justice must be served. Crimes must be punished and I'll see that they are." His words were brave, but his actions belied his cocky sentiments. He looked around for his friends, but seeing he had been left alone he slowly backed away down the street.

"They're slinking away liked whipped dogs." Freedom had joined his mother at the window. As they watched, the last of the hooligans disappeared into the night.

"We had better walk the children back to their homes," Mercy said. "The streets are dark and we don't know where those people have gone."

They decided that if they all stayed together they would be safer, so like a band of Christmas carolers, they walked through the lightly falling snow and delivered the children to their grateful parents. The three Jacksons all escorted Charlotte to her boarding house before they went home.

"This isn't over yet," said James Jackson. "Until the man who is the real killer has been caught and punished, I will be in danger, and probably many others will be in danger too."

Charlotte nodded her head in agreement as she walked into her quiet boarding house.

CHAPTER TWENTY-ONE

Searching for Answers

But evil men and seducers shall wax worse and worse, deceiving, and being deceived.

Tuesday, December 19, 1843

The lavish Christmas celebrations in New York were a surprise to Charlotte. Mrs. Richardson decorated the mantel of the boarding house parlor with pine branches and promised boarders she would offer plum pudding for the holiday meal. Austere Bostonians had often ignored Christmas, but the Dutch settlers in New York had brought very different traditions to their city. Despite all their worries about the unsolved crimes, Daniel and Charlotte were in a holiday mood. Daniel was able to send money for his mother's passage to America. Charlotte was planning for her wedding. She considered sewing a new dress for herself, but with her teaching and spending time with Daniel, she could not find the time. In the end she decided a new hat would be sufficient preparation for her wedding day. Eileen helped her choose a bonnet at one of the millinery stores on Broadway. Rowena was consulted and declared the hat too plain. She brought velvet ribbon in a deep blue to make it more festive. The three women refused to let Daniel see it before the great day arrived.

Meanwhile life in the city went on its usual course. No progress was made on solving the mysterious deaths of three women connected with brothels. Rex Hamilton continued to give speeches about purifying the city. Daniel and other reporters followed him from one corner of the city to the other and wrote many stories about him. His rival, Mayor Simpson, who was in office now, did not campaign actively. He relied on his old cronies and politicians he had helped in the past.

The routine of Rex Hamilton's speeches was always the same. A group of rough-and-ready men appeared and swiftly raised a small platform at a street corner. Then two or three well-dressed men in dark suits and top hats appeared on the stand. One of them would introduce Rex Hamilton "the next Mayor of our great city" and the speech would begin. The same sentiments were echoed over and over again. We must purify our city. We must sweep Broadway clean of the immoral women who parade up and down in fancy dresses instead of staying in their homes like virtuous wives and mothers. We must get rid of corrupt officials. Our present mayor is a disgrace to the city and to you as citizens of New York."

And often the same shouts would erupt.

"What about protecting our women?"

"What about solving all the crime in the city? All the foreign riffraff and runaway slaves are ruining the city. An honest man can't make a living."

"It's easy for you to talk about purity. We want jobs and money. You can keep your purity."

Neither Daniel nor Charlotte knew what to think about Rex Hamilton. He seemed an honorable man. He had spoken out in defense of abolition, although he was certainly not a radical. As a trustee of the Pearl Street School he was helping many of the city's community of freed slaves. But did he mean what he said? Charlotte was uneasy whenever she remembered the disparaging remarks she had overheard him make in the Van Pelt house. Was he really the man he pretended to be?

The issue of closing the "sporting houses" as he often called them, was the one that seemed closest to Hamilton's heart. He would talk on and on about sweeping "lewd women" from Broadway and closing all the brothels in the city. Was that the most important issue in the city? What about all the poverty and the lack of jobs? One evening in the boarding house parlor as they talked about Hamilton, Rowena stopped in for a visit. She looked as elegant as ever in a new gray silk dress and sounded proud and pleased when she told them she had sent her mother up in Maine enough money to buy another pig for her small farm.

After she had left, Charlotte said to Daniel. "I don't think Miss Scott would like to have all the brothels closed down. If she could vote I am sure she would vote against Mr. Hamilton. Women have so few choices. I know they say that men should take care of women, but there aren't enough men to do that for everyone. At least not enough men who will be good husbands and not beat their wives and take all their money to spend on drink."

"A bad husband is worse than no husband at all," Daniel agreed, "and women have few choices. Having a good husband, and children of your own, is surely the best thing for most women. Far better than spending life as a servant in other people's houses. And what other jobs are there for women? Very few women can be teachers. And even teachers are often poor. Two people can make their way in the world much better than one alone."

"And very few women can ever find a husband as good as the one I will soon have," Charlotte added shyly. "I am a very lucky woman. Just as my mother was lucky. Even though my father never made much money he was always kind to my mother and to all of us children."

For a short time the two of them were content to smile at each other and think about the pleasures their married life would bring. But Daniel also thought about the responsibilities he was taking on and was jolted back into thinking about the present.

"We must find out who is responsible for the brothel murders," he said. "We can't spend all our time thinking about our lives, or about politics. I must write more stories for the newspaper. The more readers I can attract, the more secure my job will be."

"One thing that occurred to me," Charlotte added, "is how the murderer chose the women he killed. They lived in three different houses on different streets. They were not related nor did they know each other, it seems. Why those three rather than others?"

"What do we know about the women?" Daniel asked, consulting his notebook. "Susan Jones came from Schenectady, New York. We know more about her than the others because we talked to her sister. Susan had a child and she had a sister who helped her."

"Polly Gladstone had a child too," Charlotte pointed out. "Do you remember that? Mrs. Brown told you Polly had a son who lives with her cousins. She also said Polly used to know a married man who kept a room for her not far from here. I wonder about Beatrice Clark. Did you hear anything about her life?

Daniel searched through his notebook. "She has always lived in New York. Mrs. Taylor has known her for years. And strangely enough she had a child too. Mrs. Taylor told me that. She said that Beatrice Clark often went to Brooklyn to visit the child. I wonder how many of the women who live in these brothels have children. Some of them are so young it is hard to think of them as mothers."

"I wonder whether Rex Hamilton knows that many of the women he wants to sweep off the streets are mothers with children to care for. I wonder whether he has ever visited a brothel and talked to some of the women. He might think differently about cleaning up the city and sweeping them away."

"Yes, I wonder whether Rex Hamilton knows anything about the women he is so eager to get rid of. Did I tell you that the first time I visited the brothel where Susan Jones lived the present Mayor of the city was also there? He certainly knew those women. He was quite friendly with Mrs. Brown. He is nothing at all like Rex Hamilton, who seems to know only the richest and most upstanding citizens."

"Why does Rex Hamilton know so much about brothels? Why does he feel so strongly about them? Most people in New York do not want to think too much about what goes on in houses like that. Do you suppose Rex Hamilton ever visited one of them?"

"Did he ever have a sister or other relative who was somehow got into trouble and was involved with one?" Daniel frowned. "Perhaps we should find out more about Mr. Hamilton. He is a relative of the Van Pelt family, isn't he? I wonder whether Eileen could tell us more about him."

The next afternoon when school was out, Charlotte walked to the Van Pelt mansion to have a talk with Eileen. The January weather was bitter cold and she had to pull her shawl around her tightly as she hurried across the slippery streets to Washington Square. Stepping into the warm, aromatic kitchen was like stepping into another world. The cook, Mrs. Shepherd, and the two housemaids, Eileen and Molly, were gathered around the kitchen table peeling potatoes and talking. They quickly asked Charlotte to sit with them and share their gossip.

"Eileen told us you were going to be married, Miss Edgerton," Molly started.

"Please call me Charlotte. I'll soon be Eileen's sister-in-law. Daniel and I are looking forward to a wedding after his mother arrives."

"You should see the beautiful hat she has ready for the wedding," Eileen added.

"And what does your young man do?" asked Mrs. Shepherd. "He works for a newspaper, does he?"

"Yes, he works for Mr. Greeley's paper, the *Tribune*. He has been busy covering the election that is coming up. I have gone to several political meetings with him where we listened to Mr. Rex Hamilton. He wants to be the new Mayor. And, as you know, he is married to one of the Van Pelt daughters. You have probably all seen him."

"Oh yes," Molly answered. "He married Miss Maria Van Pelt, the oldest of the daughters. He and his wife are often here and sometimes Mr. Hamilton is here by himself. Miss Maria is sickly and spends much of her time at her family's country home. I have helped serve them dinner many times."

"Is Mr. Hamilton a friendly man?" Charlotte asked cautiously. "Does he pay any attention to you when you serve him?"

Molly exchanged a look with the cook, but hesitated before she said anything. "He is a very noticing man and often says a friendly word to us," she finally said.

"Sometimes a bit too friendly," Eileen added tartly.

"Well, we wouldn't want to say anything about private family matters," Mrs. Shepherd's voice was stern. "We are not gossips. We don't talk about them to outsiders."

"Charlotte is not an outsider. She is my family—or almost family. And there is no harm in talking to her," insisted Eileen. "Some things should be told even if the family doesn't like it."

"What kind of things would those be?" Charlotte pressed. Maybe there was a story here that she should know.

"Susan was a good friend to me and I think she deserves to have her story told," Molly said unexpectedly.

"Susan? Do you mean Susan Jones? You knew her well when she worked here? What does she have to do with Rex Hamilton?"

Again Molly exchanged looks with the Mrs. Shepherd. Then she leaned toward Charlotte, "Mr. Hamilton was all too familiar with Susan while she was here. And him a married man! She said he just wouldn't leave her alone and kept pestering her to give him a kiss, or fetch him a book from the library, or help him tie his cravat. You know as well as I do what all that led to."

"Did she speak to Mrs. Van Pelt about it?"

"Mrs. Van Pelt? You don't suppose she would hear a word against her son-in-law, do you? Oh, she has a sharp tongue for anyone who so much as looks at her family. And as for Mrs. Hamilton, she is almost an invalid. No one would dare to say a word to her about her husband. She might fall into a fainting fit."

"No one wants to hurt Miss Maria," protested the cook weakly. "Susan was a pert young woman and she should have been a bit more careful about who she looked at. She was too free with her smiles."

"Was there ever a housemaid who could run away from a man forever? Susan did her best. But we know how it ended. And when it did Susan was out the door in no time."

"And you think Mr. Hamilton was to blame?" asked Charlotte, wondering whether this could be true of a man who talked so much about ridding the city of immorality.

"He was the one. I'm sure of it," insisted Molly. "Susan so much as said so. She told me once, when he noticed what was happening, that he would take the child and raise it as his own. But she'd have none of it. She was going to raise her child herself. Of course now look what's happened to her." Molly was close to tears.

Mrs. Shepherd interrupted "We must put these potatoes on and get the evening meal ready. We haven't all day to gossip."

"No of course not," Charlotte said hastily. "I don't mean to interfere with your work. But there is an odd thing that I noticed. All of the women who were killed had children. I wonder why that was. How many of the women who live in brothels have children?"

"There is only one person who could answer that," Eileen broke in. "Even I have heard of her, although I have only been in the city a short time. That is Madam Anastasia Denis."

"Who is she?"

The three women smiled. They all knew about Madam Denis. "She is a woman's doctor. She takes care of all sorts of women's troubles. Many a girl and many a wife too go to her when she has a problem she must get rid of. Susan went to her once, but I don't think she followed her advice."

"Well, then, I must find this Madam Denis," announced Charlotte.

CHAPTER TWENTY-TWO

Meeting the Mother's Helper

You've got to cross that lonesome valley
You've got to cross it by yourself.

Wednesday, December 20, 1843

Although both Molly and Eileen had heard of Madam Denis, neither of them knew how to find her. Rowena would be the most likely person to know that. Charlotte's first thought was to write a note and ask Rowena to pay a call the following evening, but she didn't want to wait that long. She summoned up her courage and walked to the brothel to ask, thinking as she approached the door: what would Abigail or Mrs. Ripley, my old friends from Brook Farm, think of me approaching a brothel? Life here is very different from Boston. No wonder they call New York "Sin City".

The parlor in Mrs. Brown's house was far more elegant than the one in Charlotte's boarding house. Red velvet covered the chairs, the mirror had an ornate gold frame, and above the fireplace was the picture of two young women walking in a colorful garden and smiling out at the viewer. Charlotte sank down into one of the chairs as she waited for Rowena. It was no wonder that a girl like Rowena who had grown up on a hardscrabble farm in Maine, or Polly Gladstone from the miserable Five Points slum would find this life irresistible.

Rowena came down quickly and took a chair next to Charlotte. "Has something bad happened that you would be calling on me?"

"No, I just need some information. I thought I would be brave and call on you directly. You don't mind, do you?"

"Not at all." She laughed. "So long as you do not take away business from me and the others, we are happy to be friendly with you. Most respectable women wouldn't dare to cross our threshold."

"Well, this is important. I have recently realized that the three women who have been killed all had children they were raising on their own. Someone told me that a Madam Denis would likely have known all of them because she takes care of so many of the brothel workers."

"Ah yes, Madam Anastasia Denis is a good friend to many of us. It happens quite often that a woman will find herself with child when she is in no position to take care of a baby. Madam Denis has many remedies—pills and lotions that she sells. She sometimes performs operations, and she delivers babies too, if that is what is needed. You wish to meet with her?"

"I do, because if she knew all three of the victims, she might be able to give me some idea of why they would have been chosen. Do you know where Madam Denis can be found?"

"She has an impressive house near City Hall. I'll write the address down for you. If you call on her there, I think she will talk with you or give you an appointment."

Charlotte lost no time in letting Daniel know what she intended to do.

"I'll go with you."

"Oh, no! Madam Denis is used to dealing with women. She'll be more comfortable talking to me than to a man. Besides, no doubt she would worry that you would write about her in the newspaper. For once I have an advantage over you in tracking down a story."

The address Rowena had given her was a tall brownstone house on a fashionable block of mansions. Taking care of women's problems must have been a profitable business for Madam Denis. Charlotte was ushered into a small office where she saw a tiny woman in a plain dark green dress with a lacy white collar at the neck sitting behind a desk cluttered with packets of medicines and scraps of paper. She gestured Charlotte toward a straight-backed chair in front of the desk.

After introductions, Madam Denis turned quickly to business. "Now, Miss Edgerton, what can I do for you today? Are you dealing with a serious problem that needs immediate action or are you worried about possible troubles?"

"Madam Denis, I am very lucky because I do not have a medical problem myself. What I would like from you is some information that may help to prevent another crime like the ones that have shocked our city over the past months."

"I cannot imagine how I could help you with that, but tell me what you want to know." Madam Denis had a slight French accent and a soft voice that must have been reassuring for women who were telling her about their intimate problems.

"As you probably know, three young women who work in brothels have been murdered recently. The first was Susan Jones, then Polly Gladstone, and most recently Bernice Clark. I have been investigating these crimes and I have discovered that all three of these women have children. That is rather unusual for women who lead that kind of life. I wondered if you knew them and if they are connected in any way. Perhaps you have some idea of why they might have been selected as victims."

Madam Denis was silent for several minutes while she fumbled among some papers in the drawer of her desk. Charlotte wondered whether she was looking for patients' records or trying to decide what to say. Finally she replied.

"As it happens I knew all three of these women. Several years ago Bernice Clark visited me. She suspected she was with child, but was so young and ignorant that she was not sure. I offered her the medicines and lotions that would put an end to all that worry, but she hesitated and wavered and then it was too late. She was a mother. She did not turn to me for help and I never saw her again. Until the news of her death reached me through the newspapers I had no idea what had happened to her, but she was a determined young woman and appears to have made a comfortable life for herself and her son until this horrible murder occurred.

Then a year or two later Polly Gladstone came to me when she discovered she was with child. She was a milliner, but like many young women, she could not earn enough to support herself. She found a respectable man who was attracted to her and was willing to give her gifts and pay some of her expenses. All was well until she found herself pregnant. Most women in her position want to avoid this, but she told me she was in fact eager to have a child. She sold some of her jewelry and was able to pay my fee to help deliver the child and to take some time off from her work while the baby was very young. Luckily, she had cousins who offered a home to her and the baby. Polly was able to pay them, which was a help. She lived with them for a while, but she soon returned to the city and moved into a brothel. Many women find it difficult to accept a quiet life in the country after having known the excitement of city life. I met her two or three times since then and she assured me her son was safe and thriving and that she visited him often."

Charlotte was puzzled about what the connection between the two women could have been. "Do you know whether Bernice Clark and Polly Gladstone were friends? Did they have friends in common—or enemies?"

Madam Denis frowned. "I am not privy to all the secrets of my patients. As far as I know there was no connection between the two women and I certainly know of no enemies they might have had. Things were somewhat different, however, with Susan Jones."

"How was that?"

"When Susan came to me, she was still working for a well-known family in the city. She had never worked in a brothel nor do I think she had any experience with men. She told me that a married man in the family for which she worked was responsible for her dilemma. It is not unusual of course, because many men believe anyone who works as a servant must be available to them.

"Susan was a spirited girl. She was unsure what she wanted to do, although she bought some of my famous pills designed to eliminate these problems. It seems she decided not to use the pills. Several months later she returned to see me. This time she was clearly close to having a baby. She had been dismissed from the house where she worked, but had found refuge with some friends in the city who were willing to give her shelter but would not countenance having a baby in the house."

"Were you able to help her?"

"Yes. I have a large house and can occasionally give shelter to women who need a place to birth their babies and recover. Susan stayed here for several weeks and she told me more of her story. It seems the man who had seduced her was married to one of the daughters of the house where Susan worked. He was often in the house and pursued Susan persistently until eventually she yielded. When she told him that she was with child, his reaction was unusual.

"Instead of turning his back on Susan, he demanded that if the baby should be a boy, the child be given to him. He had despaired of having a son because his wife was not well, but he was determined to have an heir. He did not want Susan, of course. She would have to leave the city forever, but he would pay for her lying in and for her care until the baby was weaned."

"Did Susan accept his offer?"

"No. She was a spunky girl—I believe that is what you Americans call it. She had a great desire to keep the baby herself and to build an independent life. When she left my house it was to visit her sister and to leave the child with her, but she herself returned to New York determined to earn enough money to support both her son and herself."

Charlotte's suspicions were completely confirmed. The circumstances fitted Rex Hamilton's life perfectly. She was beginning to understand the reason for his actions, but she had another question for Madam Denis.

"Did the father know of Susan's decision? Did he accept her choice? And why do you suggest she might have had enemies."

"Apparently he kept a watch on her while she was in the city with her friends and perhaps even while she was with me. But when she went to her sister's house, she left secretly and he was unable to track her down. If she had stayed with her sister far from the city, he would might never have discovered her. When she returned to New York, of course, it is likely that the man found out about her situation. I do not know why she returned here instead of going to a different city. Perhaps she had friends here to help her find a house where she could live. She became quite a well-known figure among the sporting girls of Broadway and sooner or later the father must have discovered her whereabouts."

"Do you think he would be angry enough to kill her? Was he the enemy you speak of?"

Madam Denis might have regretted all her talk. "I will not permit myself to speculate about such a question. I do not accuse anyone. Perhaps I have already told you too many of the secrets of my clients. The world is a very complicated place, Miss Edgerton, and none of us can judge what another person might do."

Charlotte knew this was true, but she was determined to find out who was responsible for the deaths of these women. No one would believe that a distinguished man like Rex Hamilton would commit such vicious crimes, but then no one knew the depth of his feelings about having a son. It was up to her and Daniel to discover what had happened.

CHAPTER TWENTY-THREE

Hurrah for Our New Mayor

Without promotion, something terrible happens... nothing.

Friday, December 22, 1843

Charlotte told Daniel what she had learned from Madam Denis, but neither of them could figure out a way to prove the truth of their suspicions. After two days without much progress, Daniel suggested to Charlotte that they should relax and take a walk through the busy streets. With the holidays approaching, Broadway was busier and more crowded than ever. Late in the afternoon of an unusually warm winter day they joined the throng of brightly dressed men, women and families.

As they approached P. T. Barnum's American Museum with its blazing lighted doorway and flags fluttering on the roof, Daniel said, "Today would be a good day to visit the Fiji Mermaid and see what she looks like."

The crowd swept them along and Charlotte found herself in a large room filled with exhibits of strange objects. The star attraction was a "Fiji mermaid" a small creature, quite dead, floating in liquid in a large jar.

"In the picture outside the mermaid looks alive and as big as a full grown person," Charlotte voiced her disappointment. "But this poor creature is neither alive nor quite human. The fish tail looks real enough, but the body is so hairy I can't believe she ever attracted sailors from a rock."

Daniel laughed. "This is a circus. You can't expect the exhibits to equal the delights of legend. Perhaps the mermaids of our imagination will always be more beautiful than the ones that are captured and put on display."

After laughing about the mermaid and examining the figures of famous people in the waxwork museum, Charlotte and Daniel decided they had seen enough. Outside on Broadway, they found that the entertainment continued. A group of youngsters, mostly young Africans, were playing music and dancing in the street for pennies. They were not surprised to see Freedom was among them. His dancing was so spirited that pennies were clinking into the hat in front of him.

The dancing group soon had competition from a political rally setting up across the street. A makeshift platform was quickly built and torches attached to long poles at each corner. A short, gray-haired man whose cravat was somewhat askew from his exertions in raising the platform tried to attract listeners.

"Gentlemen! Citizens of New York! I call upon you to enlist in our campaign to purify our city and make it a proud"

The sound of music interrupted his words;

Oh, sweet Sally, don't you cry for me
I'm going to Alabama, my true love for to see..

Back and forth the voices dueled until the dancing group outside the museum gave up the unequal battle, scooped up all their donations and gradually dispersed. Freedom wandered over toward the speaker's stand to listen to the candidates.

By this time the gray-haired man on the platform was introducing "Our next Mayor, Mr. Rex. Hamilton," Daniel and Charlotte saw the tall, broad-shouldered Mr. Hamilton stride to the front of the platform. He looked over the cheering crowd and raised his hand for silence.

"This great Empire City of ours will be entering a new year in another week. With a new mayor and honest politicians in City Hall, we will sweep the city clean. The city is known for its brothels and its taverns. The fancy ladies who prance down Broadway in their silks and satins do not belong here. Neither do the taverns that serve cheap gin to men and women and even children. Those we can clear away. We will close the brothels and control the taverns. They are canker sores on the body of the city. We will be known as a city of innocent women and honest men. We can look forward to the new year to bring greater prosperity for..."

"Not if we don't stop the crime in the city we can't," shouted one man from the crowd. "Why haven't the police caught the murderer who is preying on the women of our fair city?"

"Hear! Hear!" called another. "Catch the murderer." "Hang the villain." Other voices came loud and clear.

"If you elect me Mayor," Rex Hamilton was shouting above the calls of the crowd. "I promise you there will be an end to crime and immorality in this city."

Daniel was writing notes in his pad, but he paused to look at Charlotte skeptically. "If New York gets rid of immorality, it will be the first city that ever did."

"But crime? At least we could get better control of crime. With only a handful of policemen and a few volunteer watchmen, nothing will ever be done. They keep arresting the wrong people," Charlotte protested. "It seems as though the police don't know how to find real criminals."

A familiar figure, a tall man in a slouch hat walked toward them in the crowd. "Mr. Gallagher, Miss Edgerton, I am happy to see you. Are you writing the story of this rally for your newspaper? The crowd sounds very exercised today. Perhaps this is not the place for a delicate lady like yourself, Miss Edgerton."

Walt Whitman sounded calm and thoughtful among all the shouting. Charlotte assured him she was not distressed by the noisy crowd. "Tell me, do you think Mr. Hamilton will be our new mayor? Are people ready for a reformer who wants to change so many habits in the city?"

"I doubt that anyone will reform New York completely," Mr. Whitman replied. "And why should they? People here work hard. They enjoy a drink with their companions after a long day's work and a dance with a pretty girl. I celebrate the life of the common man. We do not want to be sanctimonious Puritans like the Bostonians."

Daniel was listening approvingly, but now he broke in, "But there have been terrible crimes committed here and those we need to solve. No one will be able to feel safe to relax with friends after work until we have put a stop to these threats."

Freedom had joined the group by this time and Walt Whitman turned to him. "Tell me, my boy, you have entertained people on the streets of New York and no doubt in other places too. Do you feel unsafe on our streets? Do you want a mayor who will reform the city?"

"I often feel unsafe. The color of my skin does not endear to most people in this city, but I am not so sure about wanting reform. When I listen to Mr. Hamilton who says he wants to be mayor, he sounds to me just like any other man. His voice rings out with his wants just like the men in the brothels where I play my music. I just remembered who his voice reminds me of. It is that John Smith who called out to me the other night for another song. Whether it is reform or a song, every man wants something and often it is something he would be ashamed of."

"What wise words from such a young man," said Walt Whitman, who looked at Freedom with approval. "I think I will go back to my lodging and write those thoughts into the poem I am working on. 'Every man wants something.' Very good." He tipped his hat and left.

Charlotte walked slowly back to the boarding house with Daniel. "What does it mean that Mr. Hamilton sounds like John Smith?" she wondered aloud. "Has he been visiting brothels in disguise? Is that how he got in touch with Susan? Did he find her and demand that she hand over her son? How can we ever find out the truth of what happened?"

On Christmas Day the city was quiet. Small groups of people walked to the churches where choirs were singing Christmas carols and preachers were telling the story of the first Christmas. On such a quiet, church-going day it did not seem possible that terrible crimes had been committed and at least one heartless murderer was lurking in the city.

Eileen and the other servants at the Van Pelt household were given the morning free to go to church, but she chose to spend it with Daniel and Charlotte. When she arrived at the boarding house, Charlotte could see she was upset. She replied to Charlotte's holiday greeting with an angry outburst.

"This is the blackest Christmas Day of my life! Oh, Charlotte, I have been such a fool!" and with that she began sobbing. "I was so sure that Charles meant what he said to me, but do you know what happened last night? The Van Pelts had visitors for an elegant party and who should they be but a family with a lovely daughter," her voice subsided into sobs.

"But what is that to you?"

"Molly heard them talking," Eileen wailed. "And this Miss de Witte is going to marry Charles! The engagement will be announced this week. He was telling me fairy tales when he took me on that drive. He is not going to marry me ever…ever. Why was I such a fool?"

Charlotte put her arm around the girl and tried to calm her down. "It will be all right, Eileen. You are well rid of him. He is not an honest man."

By the time Daniel arrived, Eileen had controlled her sobbing and her voice sounded almost calm.

"I have decided you are right, Daniel," she told her brother. "I should leave the Van Pelt's house. Charles Van Pelt tries to kiss me every time he catches me in the pantry or hallway. But he is becoming engaged. He never meant to marry me at all. He thinks he can just play with me because I am only a housemaid. Even though I told him I would never take another ride with him, he will not believe me. I must leave that house. But I must find a position somewhere. Where shall I turn?"

"Is there any kind of position you would like? What can you do?" asked Charlotte.

"I would like to become a teacher like you. People respect teachers. But I've not had the education you have had. How could I ever become a teacher? Working as a servant makes a girl prey to every man who comes into the house. Mrs. Van Pelt was very angry at Susan Jones and made her leave, but she was not angry at the man who interfered with Susan. Why is the woman always the one who is punished?"

"I am your brother and I must take care of you," Daniel sounded as though he was ready to take up a sword in defense of his sister.

"No," decided Eileen. "I must take care of myself. You and Charlotte will have your own lives to take care of. Besides, our mother will soon be coming to New York, won't she? We must all look after her. I will make my way no matter how the Van Pelts think they can treat me. But now I must go back to the house. It is time for the dinner service to start."

"She's a brave girl," Charlotte said to Daniel after Eileen had left. "This city has many young women who are put into positions like hers. She can either find a man to marry her and take care of her or she must put up with unwanted attentions from any man who takes a fancy to her."

"Eileen is a lively girl and she has always enjoyed going out and having a good time. She says now that she has learned her lesson, but I am worried," admitted Daniel. "Being a servant can be dangerous for a young, pretty girl. She will get tired of polishing spoons and dusting chandeliers. Someday she will be tempted by another young man who asks her to go for a ride, or a walk with him. And who knows what will come of that? In the end she is the one who will suffer. How can I stop her?"

"You were the one who told her that in America a girl did not have to be a lady born but could marry anyone. Maybe she still has a small hope that someday a rich man will marry her no matter what his mother and father want him to do."

"I no longer believe that Americans are so different from the English or the Irish. Wealthy men like Charles Van Pelt marry wealthy women here just as they do in Europe. To think otherwise is folly and you know what happens to women who stoop to folly. You remember Goldsmith's poem?

> When lovely woman stoops to folly,
>   And finds too late that men betray,
> What charm can sooth her melancholy,
>   What art can wash her guilt away?
>
> The only art her guilt to cover,
>   To hide her shame from every eye,
> To give repentance to her lover,
>   And wring his bosom—is to die."

"Oh, don't even say that! Don't ever think that! Not about Eileen or anyone. Women can extricate themselves from men like Charles Van Pelt and find a life for themselves. And a life that makes it possible to hold their heads high in any company. Rowena may be satisfied with the clothes and jewelry she enjoys, but Eileen does not want a life like that." Charlotte was indignant and at the same time filled with fear for what might happen to Eileen.

"The only thing I can do right now," Daniel admitted, "is to try to be a success at the job I have. You and I will be able to help Eileen find a place in the world where she will be happy and safe. We must start by trying to solve these crimes."

Christmas was a quiet day for Daniel and Charlotte. They had a wonderful new life to look forward to, but there were many tasks to be done before they could feel begin that life. The city they were both growing to love was not a secure place to live. They had work to do.

CHAPTER TWENTY-FOUR

Who Will Care for the Child?

The breezy call of incense-breathing morn,
The swallow twittering from the straw-built shed,
The cock's shrill clarion, or the echoing horn,
No more shall rouse them from their lowly bed.

Wednesday, December 27, 1843

Charlotte felt restless during the quiet days that followed Christmas. The Pearl Street School was closed for the week between Christmas and New Year's Day, so she had no classes to teach. She paced back and forth in her small room at the boarding house. Gray winter light streamed in the high window and a few flakes of snow drifted slowly down. Charlotte took out her pen and a sheet of paper and sat uncomfortably on the edge of the bed to write on the tiny dressing table.

Questions—1.Did Rex Hamilton know Polly Gladstone and Bernice Clark? 2. Did he know about their children? 3. Why was he campaigning to close the brothels?

231

She sighed and was staring at the paper when she heard a knock at the door. "Someone in the parlor to see you, Miss" announced the cook's young daughter. Charlotte jumped up and ran quickly downstairs hoping that Daniel had found some time to call on her.

Anne Carter, Susan Jones's sister, was standing in the parlor, clutching young Johnny by the hand. The woman looked pale and tired.

"I am sorry to bother you, Miss Edgerton, but I have come down to New York to arrange to have my sister's memorial stone placed in the churchyard. I wrote to Mrs. Richardson last week to ask whether I could rent a room here for a few days and she kindly agreed."

"I am very glad to see you again, Mrs. Carter. You look weary. Perhaps you should rest a while before you try to do anything more."

"Yes, I am afraid I've caught a dreadful cold, but I must visit the stonemason and make sure that the stone will be ready to be placed on the grave tomorrow. Would it be possible for you to go with me tomorrow to see that Susan's grave is properly marked?" Charlotte was glad to agree and Anne Carter went off to make arrangements.

The next morning when Charlotte went downstairs for breakfast, there was no sign of Mrs. Carter or Johnny. Mrs. Richardson turned to her and announced, "Your friend Mrs. Carter has sent word that she is too ill to go to the cemetery today. She would like you to visit her in her room this morning."

Charlotte found Anne Carter looking even more tired than the day before. Her hair was disordered, her brow hot with fever, and a wracking cough shook her body as she tried to talk. "Alas, I am sure I cannot go visit Susan's grave this morning. I must remain in bed and fight off this fever. My husband will be needlessly worried if I cannot return home on time tomorrow."

"Oh, indeed you must not go out into the cold weather today. The wind is blowing hard; hear how it rattles the windows. You must stay in your room and nurse your cold."

"You would be doing us a great kindness, Miss Edgerton, if you would take Johnny up there to show him his mother's grave. This may be his only chance to see it." She paused while another spasm of coughing shook her. "I have hired a carriage and a driver for today, so you and he will not be too uncomfortable." She looked pleadingly at Charlotte.

Charlotte was not eager to ride up to the cemetery on such a cold day, but Anne Carter looked so miserable and unhappy that she felt obliged to go. She put on her warmest cloak and bonnet and wrapped her face with a woolen scarf against the cold. Mrs. Carter had already bundled Johnny up so he was cocooned against the cold. Johnny was a docile little boy and like most children he loved riding in carriages where he could watch the horses and listen to the driver shouting at them. He pressed his face against the tiny window all during the trip and shouted "Look, look!" each time he saw another horse or a dog. Charlotte was glad he seemed unaware they were visiting his mother's grave.

When they saw the church by the side of the road, and the bleak churchyard with its scattered gravestones, the driver pulled the horse to the side of the road and opened the carriage door for Charlotte and the boy to get down. The wind cut like a knife and Charlotte pulled her scarf closer around her head and face as she walked to the gravesite and searched for Susan's stone. It wasn't hard to find; the sharp gray of the new stone stood out from the rest which were already becoming dim with moss and grime. The ground was broken where the stonemason's men had placed the stone. If the weather had been any colder, they would not have been able to dig in the icy soil, but the cold had not yet frozen the ground.

Charlotte stared down at the tombstone and read the words. "Susan Jones 1820-1843". There were no other words. No doubt they would have been an extra expense that Anne and her husband could not afford. And what was there to say about a woman who had lived such a life and died so young? Charlotte felt tears well up in her eyes.

The sound of a horse roused her from her reverie, as Johnny pulled at her hand and cried out "Horsie, big horsie!" A small, light buggy was standing next to the carriage they had come in. A few minutes later a tall, man strode toward them. As he came nearer, Charlotte recognized Rex Hamilton.

"Good afternoon, Mrs. Carter. I sympathize with your sorrow. I was acquainted with your sister and have come to offer my respects."

"How did you know we were here?" asked Charlotte.

"I have made it my business to watch what was going on at this grave," Rex Hamilton answered, "I need to speak to you and I have been hoping for an opportunity to do so."

"Bye, bye, horsie," piped up Johnny's voice. Charlotte turned to see the carriage she and the boy had used to come to the grave had turned and was driving off. She made a move to run after it, but Rex Hamilton reached out and gently touched her arm.

"Do not be troubled, Mrs. Carter, I dismissed your driver and will be glad to take you back to the city myself."

"You should not have done that without permission, sir. And furthermore I must tell you that I am not Mrs. Carter. I am a friend of Mrs. Carter's. She has a severe cold and was unable to come and look at the tombstone she ordered, so I have come in her place." Charlotte turned her head aside as she spoke and pulled her scarf further up her face so Hamilton would not recognize her.

Rex Hamilton drew himself up, determined to take control of the situation. "I beg your pardon for the misunderstanding. I assumed you were Miss Jones's sister. But that does not change my purpose. I am not interested in you, or Mrs. Carter. My primary interest is in the boy. I do not know how much you know about the situation, but this boy is my son and I intend to raise him as a Hamilton. I will not surrender him to his mother's disreputable family. I am willing to pay a high price to satisfy Mrs. Carter's needs, but I will not be robbed of my son."

"This is the first time I have heard it said that you were his father," Charlotte said firmly. "I know that Miss Jones and her sister have taken care of the child since he was born. Surely it will be up to his family to decide what is best for Johnny. Now please drive us back to my boarding house where Mrs. Carter is waiting for us. Johnny is getting very cold out here."

"Yes, we must not linger. Come and get into my buggy. My horse is good and we will be back in the city before long." With that Hamilton offered an arm to Charlotte, who had lifted the tired child to her shoulder, and led them back to his waiting buggy. It was a light vehicle and Rex Hamilton seemed to be an experienced driver. The horse moved swiftly over the dry, rutted roads as they sped back toward lower Manhattan. Charlotte pulled Johnny close to her side and he fell asleep. Charlotte hoped they would soon be in front of Mrs. Richardson's boarding house.

When they reached Fourteenth Street, the traffic increased and their speed slowed. Horses and carts moved slowly through the streets and Charlotte fretted that Anne Carter would be worried. Rex Hamilton, however, looked supremely confident as he explained to Charlotte.

"It's just money those country folk want. Mrs. Carter won't give me any trouble. Susan may have tricked me for a while, but she can't do anything now. Women are beginning to think they can have everything their way, but men are the ones who know best. These New York women with their fancy clothes and jewelry are the worst, but they are only women and can't think the way men do. I can show them. I'm a man and we are meant to decide how things are to be done."

"Mrs. Carter will never let you have Johnny," insisted Charlotte. "She and her husband love the boy and will never give him up."

"We'll see about that," declared Hamilton. "I can take care of my son and I can keep him in a place where no one will find him. I have money and I have friends. Does this poor woman really think she can defeat me?" With sudden determination, he turned the buggy toward the left and it clattered down the street away from the boarding house on Thomas Street.

"Where are you going? This isn't right," Charlotte was suddenly frightened.

"Don't worry. I won't hurt you or the boy. I just want him and you to be safe and where I can get hold of you both when I want you. Then we'll see how much of a fight Mrs. Carter will put up."

Before she realized where they were going, Rex Hamilton drew the buggy up in front of the Pearl Street School. He grabbed Johnny off the seat and held him firmly with one arm while he pulled Charlotte down from the buggy. She might have been able to twist away from him, but she knew he would not let go of Johnny. She had to stay with the child.

Johnny woke and started to yell as he realized he was in the stranger's arms. Hamilton reached into the pocket of his jacket and pulled out the lock to the padlocked door. He unlocked the door without letting Johnny down and then pulled Charlotte into the front hall.

"Don't be foolish enough to try to get away," he warned Charlotte. "I am going to see Mrs. Carter and talk some sense into her. I'll be back to get you and the boy later."

The heavy door swung closed behind him and Charlotte heard the padlock squeal as Hamilton pushed it firmly shut and locked it. She looked around in panic. How were they going to get away now? Would Rex Hamilton really take the boy away and hide him where Anne Carter could never find him? He was a powerful and dangerous man.

CHAPTER TWENTY-FIVE

Trapped and Afraid

As' twere a spur upon the soul,
A fear will urge it where
To go without the spectre's aid
Were challenging despair.

Wednesday, December 27, 1843

Charlotte settled Johnny on the floor. He was sobbing quietly, but so tired that he remained peaceful and watched Charlotte trustingly. She knew she had to save him somehow and give him back to the Carters. That was what Susan had wanted for him.

The first thing Charlotte did was to walk around the room and test the windows. They were set high in the walls and were securely locked. If only she could find a ladder she might be able to break the glass. Perhaps there was a ladder in the kitchen pantry, but when she walked to the door of the kitchen, she found that locked too. So was the door to Mr. Fox's office. He must have been careful to see that everything was locked before the holiday break. Discouraged, Charlotte went back to her classroom.

Johnny's eyes were closed and his face looked peaceful as he lay curled in the blanket. Carefully Charlotte dragged one of the heavy benches toward the window and climbed up on it. Still the window was out of reach and even if she could reach it, she realized, she had nothing heavy enough to break the glass.

Darkness was falling and Charlotte knew it would soon be pitch black inside. Lamps were too expensive for the classrooms, which made the room impossible to use except during daylight hours. Mr. Fox kept a supply of candles in his room for emergencies, but Charlotte had no way of getting in there to find them. She sat down on one of the benches and tried to think of how she could possibly get out before Rex Hamilton returned.

Across town...Daniel left the *Tribune* office as the sun was setting over the harbor. He drew a deep breath of frosty air and hurried to get a bite to eat before he went to see Charlotte. Although he was discouraged over their lack of progress in solving the murders, he felt that they were moving closer to finding the culprit. Rex Hamilton was clearly a suspect. If he had been bullying Susan Jones to get her baby, perhaps he was angry enough to kill.

Finishing a hasty bowl of soup, Daniel rushed down the street to Mrs. Richardson's boarding house to visit Charlotte. As soon as he knocked on the door, he realized something was wrong. Mrs. Robinson let him in, but her face was very serious and worried as she led him to the parlor.

"Have you found my boy?" were the first words he heard when the parlor door opened. It took him a minute to recognize Anne Carter standing in front of a blazing fire wringing her hands as she talked. His bewilderment must have shown on his face, because Mrs. Carter continued with her explanation.

"I was so sick this morning that Miss Edgerton took Johnny to the graveyard to make sure Susan's gravestone was properly placed. But that was hours ago and she has not returned. Where could she be?"

"How were they to get to the graveyard? They could not have walked."

"No, I had arranged to have a carriage for them. The man at the livery stable seemed honest and trustworthy. Mrs. Richardson recommended him."

"I will try to find him and see whether he returned." Daniel got directions and ran to the stable. The carriage driver was there and unworried.

"I left the young lady and the child in good hands, sir," he protested. "The gentleman who came to fetch them said he was her brother and he would drive her home in his buggy. He too wanted to see the gravestone. Paid me a handsome tip he did. I could tell he was a real gentleman."

By this time Daniel was frantic with worry. "Miss Edgerton does not have a brother here. What did this man look like?"

"He was tall and well-dressed, carried a handsome cane when he got down from the buggy. I could see by the cut of his trousers that they were made by a good tailor. As I say, he was a real gentleman."

Daniel hurried back to the boarding house to give Mrs. Carter the discouraging news. Questions flooded his mind. Could the mysterious man have been Rex Hamilton? If it was, what was he trying to do? Why was he at the graveyard? Was he hoping to take the child by force?

Daniel decided to walk to the Van Pelt house. Eileen or Molly might be able to tell him where Rex Hamilton lived. The night was very dark now and the cold weather had kept most people indoors. A light snow was beginning to fall and the streets were muffled and strangely quiet. Where could Charlotte have gone? Where would she have felt safe?

"At school," the thought flashed in his mind. Would she have taken Johnny to the school if she had a chance? It was worth trying. He turned and walked down Pearl Street. The school loomed in front of him, a darker black against the dark sky. No light shone out the windows. The street was very silent.

She can't be here, Daniel thought. The place is empty. Still, he walked toward the building and went to the door to see whether it could possibly be open. A large padlock held the door firmly shut. Daniel looked at it in despair.

He was about to turn away when he heard a faint sound. It was music. Someone was playing the piano in that dark building. Who was in there? Cautiously he put his ear against the door. There is was again—the strains of a familiar melody. He could remember singing it with Charlotte and Eileen at the oyster house.

A nation once again
A nation once again
And Ireland long a province
Be a nation once again.

Something caught in his throat. It was as though Charlotte was talking to him—sending him a message. He pounded on the door as hard as he could. "Charlotte, Charlotte. Are you there?"

There was an answering knock on the inside of the door. "Oh Daniel, Daniel. Have you really come?" The voice subsided into sobs.

By this time his pounding had attracted the attention of a watchman stationed down at the end of the block.

"Stop that racket," the man yelled. "Are you trying to break into the school?" He raised his cudgel as he approached Daniel.

"There is a woman locked inside," Daniel explained. "One of the teachers. She has a child with her." As if on cue Johnny began to cry loudly. "We must get them out."

By this time the noise was attracting a crowd. A second watchman joined his colleague and several men appeared to give suggestions. "What we need is a blacksmith to smash that padlock," said one. In just a few minutes a blacksmith was there with his heavy hammer and had soon smashed the lock.

As Daniel opened the door, he saw Charlotte standing in the hall with Johnny in her arms. They moved toward each other. "Who was it who brought you here?" he asked.

"It was Rex Hamilton. He is determined to hide Johnny away and keep Anne Carter from finding him. He thinks he has the right to take his son no matter what Susan wanted."

"He has no right to kidnap the boy," Daniel insisted and the watchmen agreed. "He must have had a key for the padlock because he is a trustee. When he comes back to get the boy, we will have proof that he kidnapped him."

The watchmen told the knot of onlookers to disperse and the blacksmith produced another padlock and fastened it to the door but left it unlocked. Daniel and the two watchmen settled themselves close to the door while Charlotte took Johnny further back. His small hand clutched her shawl but he was quiet. A small pool of light from the watchman's lantern brightened the hallway as the group waited to see what would happen next.

CHAPTER TWENTY-SIX

A Change of Fortune

It was roses, roses all the way,
With myrtle mixed in my path like mad:
The house-roofs seemed to heave and sway
The church-spired flamed, such flags they had,
A year ago on this very day.

Wednesday, December 27, 1843

Time crept by. Johnny put his head on Charlotte's shoulder and cried, asking for his mother. As Charlotte soothed him, the cries gradually subsided into sobs and then he was quiet. Daniel walked impatiently back and forth, peering out of the window at the silent street while the two watchmen stamped their feet impatiently. At last they heard the sound of a horse outside. Someone strode up the steps and they could hear the padlock clatter as it was pulled out of the lock.

"What the devil has happened to this?" muttered a voice as the padlock fell. The door opened and the tall shape of Rex Hamilton appeared in the doorway. The

245

two watchmen walked up to him and each took an arm. Daniel stepped forward and spoke to Hamilton,

"Mr. Hamilton, I accuse you of kidnapping this young woman and a child. We are going to take you to the police station to have charges brought."

"You have no right to take Johnny away from Anne Carter. You forced us to come here," added Charlotte.

"You can't do this," spluttered Hamilton. "Do you know who I am? I am a respectable man and I can explain my actions."

"You will have a chance to do so," answered a watchman. "We are going to the police station where you all will have a chance to give an account of what happened."

"You can't take me to a police station," shouted Hamilton. "I am soon to be mayor of New York City. You cannot treat me as a common criminal. This woman is lying. She teaches in this African school. What kind of woman would do that? Spending all her time with these people. Pretending they can be educated just like white children. What do women know?"

The watchmen were looking more and more doubtful as Rex Hamilton continued to rant, but Daniel was outraged. He turned to the watchmen.

"You must take Mr. Hamilton to the police station. I will bring the woman who brought the complaint and you can question her there. In this country the law is equal for all. I will write a story for the *Tribune* about how this matter was dealt with."

The watchmen went to the police station with Rex Hamilton, while Daniel and Charlotte took Johnny and hurried to the boarding house to find Anne Carter. It was almost eight o'clock by this time and the evening meal was just finishing at the boarding house. Mrs. Richardson was happy to give Johnny something to eat and watch the boy until Mrs. Carter returned.

The streetlights had been lit and the police station was lighted inside by several oil lamps. As Daniel and the two women hurried to the front desk, Rex Hamilton jumped up from where he had been sitting. He pushed past the watchmen and accosted Mrs. Carter.

"You have been keeping my son from me. You have been hiding him away just because his foolish mother wanted it. I demand that you give him to me. I will make it worth your while and you will not be troubled by him again."

Mrs. Carter drew herself up, although she scarcely reached his shoulders. "Johnny is my sister's child. I will not let him be taken from me. Susan wanted me and my husband to keep him. What right do you have to claim him now? How do I even know you are his father? You have never done anything to help him."

"How dare you talk like that, woman?" Hamilton was shouting now. "You look just like Susan with her airs and fancy ideas. I am a wealthy man and I tell you I will have that boy. You and your pitiful husband cannot keep him from me. Do you know who I am?"

"I am a mother to Johnny, and my husband is a good father to him. Susan wanted to raise him on her own and now that she is gone, I will do it for her."

Rex Hamilton's face was turning red and his voice trembled with anger. "Impudent woman! I will silence you just as I silenced Susan. She thought she could get her way, but no woman has a right to oppose her man." He lunged toward Mrs. Carter and reached out as if to seize her by the throat.

Daniel and the watchmen grabbed his arms and restrained him but he was almost mad with rage and wrestled with all three of them. "We will not have petticoat rule! Women must submit to men. We know how to guide and lead them. I proved that to Susan—and to Polly too who tried the same trick. And I'll kill you too," he shouted at Anne Carter.

Charlotte took Anne Carter's shoulders and pulled her back against the wall. The woman was shaking and tears streaked her face. "He is the one who killed Susan. How could he do that? He's a monster. I'd die before I'd let him take Johnny."

Even the police were shaken by Hamilton's story. They took him into custody, deciding to hold him until a judge could come the next morning and determine what formal charges should be laid.

The next morning Daniel went to the Hall of Justice to find out what more information the hearing would bring out. Judge Potter, one of the few court offices available during the holiday season had been hastily summoned by one of the policeman. Daniel recognized Judge Potter and followed the large man as he advanced ponderously up the stairs of the massive building and sat down at a massive desk in the hearing room. The two policeman and Rex Hamilton stood before the judge while Daniel and a small cluster of newsmen tried to look inconspicuous along the side walls of the chamber.

"Do you deny that you brought Miss Edgerton and the child to the Pearl Street School and locked them in the building?"

"No, I admit I did that. I had to. The boy is my son and I have a right to take him. His mother was trying to keep him from me. I told her I would find him and take him. She had no right to hide him away with her sister. She laughed at me and said I would never have him. She laughed!" His face became distorted with rage. "She had no right to do that. I had to silence her. I soon put an end to her laughter."

"Did you kill Susan Jones?" asked the judge.

"I didn't mean to kill her. I seized her and shook her, but she kept laughing. The woman should not have laughed at me. I have a right to my son. I had to stop her."

"And what of Polly Gladstone?" the judge continued relentlessly. "Do you admit you knew her too?"

"Of course I knew her. I kept her in comfort for more than a year. For a long time she was content to be my mistress and take the pretty clothes and jewels I bought her, but she wanted more. When she realized she would have a child, she wanted me to publically acknowledge her and let her raise my child. How could I do that? It would ruin my career. It was the child I wanted—not the woman. The child could easily be passed off as being born to my wife. My wife never disobeys me, but the Gladstone woman was stubborn. She thought she could get away from me and keep the child."

Rex Hamilton showed the strain of standing before the judge and reciting his history. He ran his hand through his hair and clenched his fists as he waved them in the air. "Women are too independent these days! They have no sense. They think they can run their own lives. My wife at least is a real woman who never stands against me. We must get rid of these wicked hussies who walk the streets and tempt good men to evil deeds. I was never an evil man. I never meant to harm anyone. I only want what is rightfully mine."

The judge took pity on the stricken man and ended the questioning. "I must order your arrest for murder. You will be held in custody, but you may communicate with your lawyer and your family. We need not take this any further this morning."

Daniel's next story created a sensation when it appeared in the *Tribune*:

Mayoral Candidate Charged with Murder

How the mighty have fallen! Rex Hamilton, a well-known citizen and candidate for Mayor of New York, has confessed to murder in the mysterious deaths of two sporting girls in the city. In a twist reminiscent of a novel by Charles Dickens, this well-known and respected man has admitted that he was the father of children born to these women. In an effort, applauded by some, to control the lives of his children and keep them away from the influence of their mothers, he attempted to take the boys by force. Tragically, when the women resisted his wishes, his temper overcame him and, as he has confessed, he strangled both of them. Mr. Hamilton is now arranging legal counsel to represent him at his upcoming trial. There is no question but that the public will spend many hours arguing about the rights of both parents in a case as complicated and unsavory as this one is. Information about the death of Beatrice Clark has not been released, but there is reason to believe that Mr. Hamilton also has knowledge about that. This public will be awaiting further details in this newspaper as they become available.

It was some days before Daniel learned further details about the death of Beatrice Clark. Rex Hamilton refused to see him, but a few days after the arrest, Hamilton's lawyer was willing to speak about the case. Daniel went to the well-appointed office of Hamilton's lawyer, Otis Harrison, who gave a few details about the case.

Mr. Harrison, a tall, grave man with white hair and an authoritative manner, spoke slowly. He sounded, Daniel thought, as though he were addressing a jury rather than a single journalist.

"My client, Mr. Hamilton, did not know this woman Beatrice Clark. He visited the brothel in which she worked with the laudable purpose of influencing some of the women, and perhaps their clients, to abandon the sinful paths on which they were embarked. When he attempted to inject a more moral and spiritual tone to the scene, however, he was ignored and indeed insulted by that young poet, Lawrence Abingdon. He left the house, but remained troubled by the encounter."

Otis Harrison paused to look at some papers he was holding, as though seeking further confirmation of the facts, but then he turned back to Daniel.

"The morning following this visit, Mr. Hamilton decide to return to the brothel to see whether he could influence some of the women in the sober light of day. Outside the house he encountered this woman, Beatrice Clark, who was waiting for a carriage to take her to Brooklyn. When Mr. Hamilton spoke to her kindly, but seriously, about the importance of giving up the life she was living, the impudent woman argued with him. In fact, she laughed at him and said she was quite satisfied with her life. Such an answer to Mr. Hamilton's well-intended remarks, rather enraged my client, who has been under severe strain in recent months."

"And in his range Mr. Hamilton attacked Miss Clarke?" Daniel was eager to get to the point.

"I am afraid so. His reason was quite overturned. There is no other way to explain such an uncharacteristic response. Without realizing what he was doing, he seized Miss Clarke roughly and unfortunately she died."

"She was strangled, just as his other two victims were."

Mr. Harrison coughed and was silent for a time. "Well, yes, I am afraid that Mr. Hamilton was becoming wilder and less controlled. He did indeed strangle Miss Clarke and move her body to the back of the house where it was discovered. His actions after that were those of a madman. The kidnapping of Miss Edgerton and the boy were the unfortunate result of his mental collapse." Mr. Harrison looked sorrowful as he finished and fell silent.

Newspapers throughout the city seized upon the story and the public demanded all of the details. Judge Potter ruled that Rex Hamilton should be kept in custody until a trial could be arranged. All of his plans to be a leading citizen of the city crumbled around him.

Anne Carter stayed in the city only long enough to see Rex Hamilton indicted. After thanking Charlotte and Daniel as well as Rowena for the help they had given her, she took Johnny and went back to Schenectady where she hoped he would find a peaceful life

CHAPTER TWENTY-SEVEN

The Concert

Ring out the old, ring in the new,
Ring, happy bells, across the snow:
The year is going, let him go;
Ring out the false, ring in the true.

Monday, January 1, 1844

On the day after Rex Hamilton's arrest, John Fox and the Board of Trustees held an emergency meeting to decide what to do about the planned New Year's Day concert. Charles Ray was appointed chair of the Board and he urged that the concert be given as scheduled.

"The best way to protect the school from scandal," he insisted, "is to demonstrate to the public that our work is going well. Neither the children nor the teachers of this school have been disgraced, so we must hold up our heads and show our value to the community. My own church, the Bethesda Congregational Church is prepared to host the concert despite the unfortunate recent events."

New Year's Day dawned bright and sunny. Charlotte worried that the scandal reported in the newspapers might dampen enthusiasm for the concert, but instead the church soon attracted a larger than expected crowd. Notices about the concert had been sent to friends and supporters of the school and news was spread through newspapers and church bulletins. The newspaper stories about Rex Hamilton had attracted many curious spectators, but Charlotte was glad to see that it was not only curiosity seekers who formed the crowd.

She noticed Margaret Fuller come in with Mr. and Mrs. Greeley and Lawrence Abingdon was there with his friend Walt Whitman. The church was filled with a low murmur of voices which died away when Mercy Jackson led the first group of children to the front of the church. At a signal from her, the children began to sing a cappella:

Swing low, sweet chariot,
Comin' for to carry me home;
Swing low, sweet chariot,
Comin' for to carry me home.

With that first song the audience was captivated. Even those who had come only to scoff at the idea of black children performing for an audience of city leaders had to admit that the entertainment was first rate. Daniel sat at the back of the audience scribbling notes for the story he planned to write. He noticed the nodding heads and approving smiles as the concert continued. When the time came to end it, John Fox and Charles Ray stood together at the front to announce that the children would sing a hymn in memory of the unfortunate women who had died in the city.

"None of us understand what drives a person to commit hideous crimes," Charles Ray pronounced. "We all stand together in pity for those who have suffered and died at the hands of another. No human being, no matter how sinful her life, is beyond the reach of forgiveness. May God have mercy on their souls and on the souls of all of us." He raised his arm and the children sang:

God of mercy and compassion,
Look with pity upon me,
Father, let me call Thee Father,
'Tis Thy child returns to Thee.

After the concert people were in no hurry to leave. Many in the audience wanted to meet the children and to talk about the school. Charlotte was glad to have a chance to speak to Margaret Fuller.

"Thank you, Miss Fuller, for encouraging me to try to arrange this concert. I am sure that it will be of great benefit to the children and the school."

"You and your colleagues have done all the work to make this a success," Miss Fuller replied. "And I am pleased to tell you that Mr. Greeley has suggested that I write an article for the *Tribune* about the success of the school and other efforts to educate the freed slaves. As you know, he is a firm supporter of the abolitionist cause as is his wife. Let me introduce you to Mrs. Greeley, whose hospitality I have enjoyed ever since I moved to New York."

Lawrence Abingdon and Walt Whitman came over to talk with them. Whitman was especially pleased with the generous words Charles Ray has spoken about the three murdered women.

"I honor all human beings," pronounced Walt Whitman in his authoritative voice. "Why should we not respect the prostitutes who earn their living in the city? I have written a poem about these women:

Not till the sun excludes you, do I exclude you;
Not till the waters refuse to glisten for you, and the leaves to
rustle for you, do my words refuse to glisten and rustle for
you.

The evening had been a triumph for the school and its future at last seemed secure. Charlotte and Mercy Jackson could return to their work without worrying about more parents taking the children out of school.

CHAPTER TWENTY-EIGHT

A Joyous Celebration

My heart is like a rainbow shell
That paddles in a halcyon sea;
My heart is gladder than all these
Because my love is come to me.

Saturday, March 16, 1844

The March sun was struggling through the clouds as
Agatha Gallagher tied on her bonnet and went
downstairs to meet her son. Charlotte was already in the
parlor sitting demurely on the sofa clutching a small
bunch of violets that Daniel had presented to her. The
three of them stepped outside into the nippy air and
walked toward St. Patrick's church.

Charlotte had expected to be married at City Hall, but
in deference to Agatha, soon to be her mother-in-law,
she had agreed to be married by a priest. Her father
would have been scandalized to hear of a Catholic
wedding, but he had died several years earlier and would
never know. And her mother, Charlotte knew, would

support whatever choice she made trusting her to find her own path. Charlotte herself was indifferent to who might preside at the marriage ceremony. She and Daniel were so sure of their love they felt they could be generous in making concessions to others.

St. Patrick's Church was small and dark. One panel of stained glass window cast colored light on the tile floor, but the other narrow windows were simple glass. It would take years to afford imported stained glass for all the windows. Eileen joined them at the back of the church and the small party walked up the aisle to where a priest wearing silk vestments stood before an altar lit with two wax candles. There were only a few people in the pews. The Jackson family were all there, beaming proudly at their friends, a few of the children from Charlotte's school, and Molly and Mrs. Shepherd from the Van Pelt house who wanted to see Eileen and Charlotte in their new bonnets.

Eileen Gallagher served as maid of honor, and James Jackson acted as best man for Daniel. The ceremony was brief, the wedding party signed the register, the priest blessed them, and it was over.

At the Pearl Street School the group found a simple celebratory meal laid out. Mr. Fox has decided the larger classroom could be used to mark the occasion and Freedom had prepared the children for a concert. Lawrence Abingdon and Rowena Scott joined them, a rather unconventional pair of wedding guests, but welcomed by all.

The children had learned a new song to sing to them:

'Tis the gift to be simple, 'tis the gift to be free
'Tis the gift to come down where we ought to be,
And when we find ourselves in the place just right,
'Twill be in the valley of love and delight.

The city was quiet, and Charlotte was glad to see Mercy Jackson relaxed and smiling at last. She had been anxious for so long that it seemed she had forgotten how to smile. Now, however, her broad, happy smile was back and her rich, contralto voice joined the children in singing.

Eileen had left the Van Pelt family service. Even though she had not taken part in the action that brought disgrace to Rex Hamilton and humiliation to his wife and family, she felt too close to it to be comfortable in their home. Instead of entering service in another household, Eileen was going to work as an assistant at the Pearl Street School. There she would help out in classes, which were growing larger now that the school was well known. She would learn to be a teacher by observing Charlotte and Mercy as they taught.

Daniel had told his sister that she could find a successful life in America by marrying a man of substance, but now she realized she would rather carve out a life for herself. She wanted to come to marriage, as Charlotte had, as an independent woman who had forged her own path. She and Daniel were entering married life as equals, sharing their dreams and working toward a common goal. Eileen was determined to become a teacher before she considered marriage and a family of her own.

Epilogue

During the weeks while winter turned into spring in New York and Charlotte and Daniel entered their new life as a married couple, Rex Hamilton was also slipping into a new and unexpected life. Instead of being an honored candidate for mayor of the city, he was only another prisoner lost in the gray prison of the Tombs. His wife had gone to her grandmother's home in Tarrytown and had no plans to return to the city anytime soon. Rex was shunned even by his fellow prisoners, left alone day after day in his cell to think about the strange compulsion that made him attack vulnerable women. Deserted by his family, Rex had only two faithful visitors. One was the pastor of his church, who came to pray with him and to pierce the armor Rex had built up around himself. "Pride goes before destruction," Pastor Smoot reminded him. "a man has no right to destroy the lives of others no matter how great his anger. But you must pray to have the evil taken from your heart." Rex found it difficult to pray. His anger at the women who would not let him have his way remained strong. He turned Pastor Smoot away with harsh words.

His other visitor was the pale young poet Lawrence Abingdon, who despite his sympathy with the prostitutes on whom Rex had preyed, still had compassion for the man. All his life Lawrence had struggled to find the common strain that tied him to other men. His strange, haunting poetry presented a world view that was difficult for others to appreciate, but he and Rex shared a sense of estrangement from the ordinary world. The poem Lawrence had quoted as applying to Rex applied to himself as well:

> *From childhood's hour I have not been*
> *As others were; I have not seen*
> *As others saw; I could not bring*
> *My passions from a common spring.*
> *From the same source I have not taken*
> *My sorrow; I could not awaken*
> *My heart to joy at the same tone;*
> *And all I loved, I loved alone.*
> *Then- in my childhood, in the dawn*
> *Of a most stormy life- was drawn*
> *From every depth of good and ill*
> *The mystery which binds me still:*
> *From the torrent, or the fountain,*
> *From the red cliff of the mountain,*
> *From the sun that round me rolled*
> *In its autumn tint of gold,*
> *From the lightning in the sky*
> *As it passed me flying by,*
> *From the thunder and the storm,*
> *And the cloud that took the form*
> *(When the rest of Heaven was blue)*
> *Of a demon in my view.*

The two men found a bleak comfort in confronting their demons together. Even though Rex expected to be hanged before the year was out, he felt more at peace than he had for years. His ambitions had all failed, but gradually the rage that had tormented him for so long had dwindled away. He understood at last that the world was not his to control.

Afterword: Could that really happen?

Some of the characters who appear in *Death Visits a Bawdy House* are historical figures who were in New York during the time that my fictional characters, Charlotte and Daniel, lived there. I have tried to present them in a way that is true to what they were really like. Although I have invented dialog for some of them, including Margaret Fuller and Walt Whitman, I have based their words on what I know of their characters and ideas. After several years spent working on this book, they have come to seem very real to me and I hope the words I have attributed to them would not offend them.

Bronson Alcott does not appear in *Death Visits a Bawdy House*, but he is mentioned several times. He is now perhaps best remembered as the father of Louisa May Alcott, but during the 19th century he was an important

267

educational theorist, writer and philosopher. He believed that children should not be taught to repeat what the teacher told them but encouraged to think and speak for themselves. He started the Temple School in Boston, but it was considered too radical for many parents. When he enrolled a Negro child in the school, so many students were withdrawn that the school failed.

Margaret Fuller was one of the most influential American writers and journalists of the early nineteenth century. Born in Massachusetts, she was a friend of Ralph Waldo Emerson, Henry Thoreau and others of their circle. Her most famous book *Women in the Nineteenth Century* influenced later feminists including Elizabeth Cady Stanton and Susan B. Anthony. During the 1840s she traveled in the United States and Europe as a journalist for Horace Greeley's newspaper the *Tribune*.

Horace Greeley founded his influential newspaper, *New York Tribune*, in 1841. The newspaper soon had the largest circulation of any American newspapers and brought about the popularity of the daily press. His newspaper was largely an expression of his own views and he was a friend to the New England transcendentalists including Ralph Waldo Emerson and Margaret Fuller. He was an abolitionist and a political activist who popularized the slogan "Go West young man!" Later in life he developed political ambitions and ran for president in 1872, an election which he lost in a landslide.

Edgar Allen Poe does not appear in the text of *Death Visits a Bawdy House*, but his spirit hovers over the book in the person of Lawrence Abingdon. His real life story was not at all like the life of Lawrence Abingdon, but his melancholy awareness of the pain of love and loss were similar. The quotations from Abingdon's poetry in chapters 4, 8, 18 and in the Epilogue are actually from Poe's work.

Charles Bennett Ray was born free in Falmouth, Massachusetts in 1807. He started his career as a boot maker, but after a religious conversion decided to become a Methodist minister. He enrolled at Wesleyan University in Connecticut as the college's first black student but enrollment was cancelled after only a few months because other students protested against his admission. This led him to move to New York City in 1831 where he became the editor of the newspaper *Colored American*. He was politically active in working to abolish slavery and to secure voting rights for black Americans. As a conductor on the Underground Railroad, he helped fugitives escape from slavery and he worked with the Quaker Isaac Hopper to assist fugitives. He was a strong supporter of education for Black children. In 1845 he established the Bethesda Congregational Church.

Walt Whitman, one of the major American poets of the 19th century, was a young journalist during the 1840s. Born on Long Island in 1819, he had left school at the age of eleven and worked as a printer and typesetter on several newspapers during his teenage years. He read widely and soon began writing poetry and articles. He was always politically active and generally supported liberal social position; he opposed the extension of slavery to new states and he sympathized with women driven into prostitution because of economic necessity. His ability to sympathize with social outcasts is shown in these lines from his "To a Common Prostitute" quoted in Chapter 27. *"Not till the sun excludes you do I exclude you,/Not till the waters refuse to glisten for you and the leaves to rustle for you, do my words refuse to glisten and rustle for you."* In 1846 he became the editor of the *Brooklyn Daily Eagle,* but he soon began concentrating on writing poetry rather than journalism. He published the first edition of *Leaves of Grass* in 1855.

Note on prostitution in NYC in the 1840s.: The period between 1800 and 1850 was a time of dramatic commercial growth and wide social turmoil in New York City. The colonial tradition of family farms and stable communities could no longer support the growing American population. More and more young people were moving to cities to find work in the factories, stores, or offices that clustered in the city after the opening of the Erie Canal in 1825. Young men could find work more easily than women, who were often limited to working as domestic servants, dressmakers, or in small factories. Pay was lower for women than for men, so many women turned to part-time or fulltime prostitution to make ends meet.

Prostitutes could prosper in the early years of the century because the brothel business was run by women. Successful brothel owners had far more freedom than women who worked as domestic servants or were married to men who controlled their lives and money. Landlords often encouraged brothels to rent their property because their rental income was usually stable and growing in a market where constantly rising rents meant many small tradespeople could not afford to pay.

Prostitution was not a crime in the city, although prostitutes could be arrested for vagrancy or disorderly conduct. The number of prostitutes is uncertain and estimates range from 3000 to 10,000. The only agreement seems to be that they were very visible and many New Yorkers as well as visitors to the city remarked on the large number of prostitutes in the city. Many of them were very young; the legal age of consent for sex was 10, and many girls of 12 or 14 were prostitutes either to help support their families or to achieve freedom from them.

Most prostitutes in the 1840s operated without pimps and lived far more independent lives than most women at that time. It wasn't until the 1850s and 1860s that widespread violence against brothels, by roving bands of men conducting "sprees" led to the need for protection; eventually male pimps began to take over many of the brothels and control the prostitutes. Male political figures such as precinct leaders also found that taking money to protect prostitutes from violence and harassment was a lucrative source of funds to maintain their political power, so they also became power brokers in the business of prostitution.

Note on the free black community. New York City attracted many free blacks in the years before the Civil War. After slavery was abolished in the state in 1827, many former slaves found it easier to live in New York than in Southern states where they were frequently challenged to prove their free status. By 1840, there were more than 16,000 free blacks in the city, although only 90 men in the group were allowed to vote because of stringent property requirements. Blacks still faced many obstacles as jobs were few and many had very little education. Former slaves who were lucky enough to have been prepared for a trade were sometimes able to find a job or start a business; a few became wealthy. But for the majority, who had been hampered by laws in the South that made it illegal to teach slaves to read, finding economic security was difficult.

During the early years of the 19th century, most organizations for free blacks and former slaves used the word 'African' in their names, emphasizing their ties with the continent from which their ancestors had come.

Many activists, however, were opposed to the colonization schemes proposed by some white anti-slavery supporters who proposed sending former slaves back to some location in Africa. Black leaders decided that the word "colored" would emphasize both their distinct identity and their ties to America as well as their determination to remain in the country. It was a word they preferred to being called Africans and many organizations used the word in their titles.

Note on police and watchmen in New York City: At the beginning of the 1840s, New York City did not have an official police force. Part-time watchmen protected the city from crime, but as the city grew, citizens recognized that this traditional protection was not enough. The idea of forming a police force became a controversial political question as successive mayors and city councilmen argued over who should appoint and control the safety officers. During the time covered in this story, a few police officers had been appointed, but it was not until 1845 that a professional police force was formed and law enforcement as we know it today began.

Sources of Quotations in the Text

Chapter 1
"Mannahatta" by Walt Whitman.

Chapter 2
"The Frail Fair" originally published in the *Whip*, August 6, 1842, quoted in *The Flash Press: Sporting Male Weeklies in 1840s New York* by Patricia Cline Cohen, Timothy J. Gilfoyle, and Helen Lefkowitz Horowitz in association with the American Antiquarian Society (Univ. of Chicago Press 2008).

"In the Graveyard" by McDonald Clarke. http://www.poemhunter.com/poem/in-the-graveyard-2/. Clarke was a popular 19th century poet who was admired by Walt Whitman and many other writers.

Chapter 3
Quotation from Bronson Alcott's *Table Talk* p. 57 (Google Books).

Chapter 4
"The Raven" by Edgar Allan Poe.
"The Haunted Palace" by Edgar Allan Poe.

Chapter 5

"*Ye of the coarser sex . . .* " from *Poems* by T. Augustus Forbes Leith.

Chapter 6

"The Bard of Armagh" an Irish ballad often attributed to Patrick Donnelly.

Caliban's speech from *The Tempest*: Act 3, Scene 2.

"A Nation Once Again" An Irish Rebel Song, written by Thomas Davis.

Chapter 7

"The Prisoner of Chillon" Lord Byron.

Quotation from Dickens in *American Notes.*

Chapter 8

"The Ruined Maid" by Thomas Hardy.

"To Isadore" Edgar Allan Poe.

"The Lamb" William Blake.

Chapter 9

"*That laughing eye...*" from *The Tenant of Wildfell Hall* by Anne Bronte p. 127 (Google Books).

Chapter 10

"*We have made...*" Bible. Isaiah 28:15 quoted by William Lloyd Garrison in a resolution adopted by the Antislavery Society (27 January 1843).

"*Twinkle, twinkle...*" from "The Star" by Jane Taylor.

Chapter 11

"Golden lads and girls..." from *Cymbeline* by William Shakespeare, Act IV, Scene 2.

"The Lord is my shepherd" Psalm 23; arranged by Francis Rous (1650).

Chapter 12

"Nobody knows..." African American spiritual.

"The Little Black Boy" by William Blake.

Chapter 13

"If I could have..." *Autobiography* by Mark Twain, p. 175 (Google Books). Text is slightly edited.

"Buffalo gals..." American folk song.
http://www.balladofamerica.com/music/indexes/songs/buffalogal/

Chapter 14

"If you have knowledge..." Margaret Fuller. BrainyQuote.com, Xplore Inc, 2015. http://www.brainyquote.com/quotes/quotes/m/margar etfu131958.html, accessed January 8, 2015.

"Ho! The Car Emancipation..." Gac, Scott. *Singing for Freedom: The Hutchinson Family Singers and the Nineteenth-Century Culture of Reform.* p. 249. (Yale Univ. Pr. 2007).

Chapter 15

"Keep your face.." Walt Whitman. BrainyQuote.com. Xplore Inc, 2015. 9 January 2015. http://www.brainyquote.com/quotes/quotes/w/waltwhi tma384665.html

"Camptown Races" a minstrel song by Stephen C. Foster.

"Swing low, sweet chariot..." a spiritual written by Wallis Willis, a Choctaw freedman who lived in Oklahoma.

Chapter 16

"How do I love thee..." Sonnet 34 by Elizabeth Barrett Browning.

"Sad the bird that sings alone..." An old Irish lament translated into English by Charlotte Brooke in *Reliques of Irish Poetry* (1789).

Chapter 17

"He'll come home, he'll not forget me, for his word is always true". Stephen Foster from *Melodies of Stephen C. Foster* (Google Books) p. 280.

Chapter 18

And why beholdest thou the mote that is in thy brother's eye, but considerest not the beam that is in thine own eye? Bible. Matthew 7:3.

"I dreamt I dwelt..." a popular aria from *The Bohemian Girl*, an 1843 opera by Michael William Balfe, with lyrics by Alfred Bunn.

"In visions of the dark night..." from "A Dream" by Edgar Allan Poe.

"Blest are the pure, whose hearts are clean" a hymn with words by Isaac Watts circa 1710.

Chapter 19

"Hope is the thing with feathers..." poem by Emily Dickinson.

Chapter 20

"Courage..." Mark Twain. BrainyQuote.com. Xplore Inc, 2015. 9 January 2015. http://www.brainyquote.com/quotes/quotes/m/marktwain138540.html

Should old acquaintance be forgot,/ and never brought to mind? "Auld Lang Syne" by Robert Burns (1788).

The gospel train is coming,/I hear it just at hand, Traditional African-American spiritual.

"Columbia, the gem of the ocean" attributed to Thomas á Becket, Sr. (1843) in Paul Holsinger, editor, *War and American Popular Culture: A Historical Encyclopedia,* Greenwood Publishing Group, 1999, p. 67.

Chapter 21

"But evil men and seducers" Bible 2 Timothy 3:13.

Chapter 22

"You've got to cross..." traditional gospel hymn.

Chapter 23

"*Without promotion...*" "P. T. Barnum."
BrainyQuote.com. Xplore Inc, 2015. 9 January 2015.
http://www.brainyquote.com/quotes/quotes/p/ptbarnu
m539959.html

"*Oh! Susanna, do not cry for me;/I come from Alabama, wid my Banjo on my knee.*" Minstrel song by Stephen Foster.

Chapter 24

"*The breezy call of incense-breathing morn,*" Thomas Gray "Elegy in a Country Graveyard".

Chapter 25

"*As' twere a spur upon the soul,*" Emily Dickinson LXVI.

Chapter 26

It was roses, roses all the way,
With myrtle mixed in my path like mad:
The house-roofs seemed to heave and sway
The church-spired flamed, such flags they had,
A year ago on this very day.
"The Patriot" by Robert Browning.

Chapter 27

"*Ring out wild bells...*" Alfred Lord Tennyson from "In Memoriam" CVI.

Swing low, sweet chariot, a spiritual written by Wallis Willis, a Choctaw freedman who lived in Oklahoma.

"God of mercy and compassion,/Look with pity upon me," http://biblehub.com/library/various/the_st_gregory_hy mnal_and_catholic_choir_book/no_134_god_of_mercy.h tm

Not till the sun excludes you, do I exclude you; Walt Whitman "To a Common Prostitute".

Chapter 28

"My heart is like a rainbow shell" Christina Rosetti "A Birthday".

'Tis the gift to be simple, 'tis the gift to be free A Shaker hymn written by Elder Joseph Brackett.

Epilogue

"From childhood's hour I have not been" Edgar Allen Poe "Alone"

www.ingramcontent.com/pod-product-compliance
Lightning Source LLC
Chambersburg PA
CBHW051417170626
46809CB00006B/2204